*As Terese smoothed her
hair into place, the image
of Hunter Coltrane flashed
through her mind. The image of
Hunter Coltrane with her...*

"Now *that's* a pipe dream," she muttered to herself.
And no one knew it better than Terese.

Because Hunter Coltrane was handsome enough
to stop traffic, leaving her with little doubt that she
wasn't the kind of woman who would so much as
turn his head.

Plain—that's what she was. It was an irrefutable
fact—Terese Warwick was a plain Jane. The kind
of plain Jane who didn't attract even moderately
attractive men on her own merits, let alone men
like Hunter Coltrane.

"And don't you forget it!" she commanded her
reflection as if it were another person.

Then she told herself to just be glad she was going
to get to meet her nephew.

She'd have to work on erasing the lingering mental
image of her nephew's father. The rugged image
that had thing

notice.

Just the way t

VICTORIA PADE

is a native of Colorado, where she continues to live and work. Her passion—besides writing—is chocolate, which she indulges in frequently and in every form. She loves romance novels and romantic movies—the more lighthearted the better—but she likes a good, juicy mystery now and then, too. She enjoyed being included in the LOGAN'S LEGACY series because it gave her the chance to revisit the appeal of the cowboy hero—one of her favorite kinds of macho men.

LOGAN'S LEGACY

FOR LOVE AND FAMILY
VICTORIA PADE

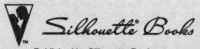
Silhouette Books

Published by Silhouette Books
America's Publisher of Contemporary Romance

Special thanks and acknowledgment are given to Victoria Pade for her contribution to the LOGAN'S LEGACY series.

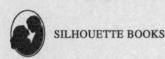 SILHOUETTE BOOKS

ISBN 0-373-61387-3

FOR LOVE AND FAMILY

Visit Silhouette Books at www.eHarlequin.com

Printed in U.S.A.

Be a part of

$\mathscr{L}$OGAN'S $\mathscr{L}$EGACY

*Because birthright has its privileges
and family ties run deep.*

**When a shy but beautiful teacher fell for him,
he had to decide whether he was ready to
love again....**

Hunter Coltrane: A widower with a sick little
boy, Hunter was reluctant to open his heart to love.
But then sweet and beautiful Terese entered his life,
and he couldn't deny the feeling growing inside him.
Maybe he *could* give love a second chance....

Terese Warwick: Terese hadn't had much luck
with men until she met Hunter and his adorable
son and instantly warmed to them. They were the
loving family she'd always wanted, but Hunter had
a damaged heart. Could she break through his old
wounds and find love?

Bachelors galore! With the upcoming charity
bachelor auction, love was in the air at Portland
General, but did someone want to ruin the
Children's Connection's good name?

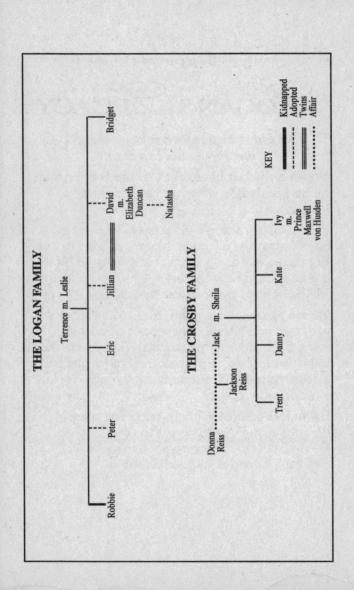

THE LOGAN FAMILY

Terrence m. Leslie

Robbie — Peter — Eric — Jillian ══ David — Bridget
                                   m.
                              Elizabeth
                              Duncan

Natasha

THE CROSBY FAMILY

Donna Reiss ·········· Jack m. Sheila

Jackson Reiss

Trent — Danny — Kate — Ivy
                              m.
                              Prince
                              Maxwell
                              von Husden

KEY

▬▬▬	Kidnapped
– – –	Adopted
═══	Twins
·········	Affair

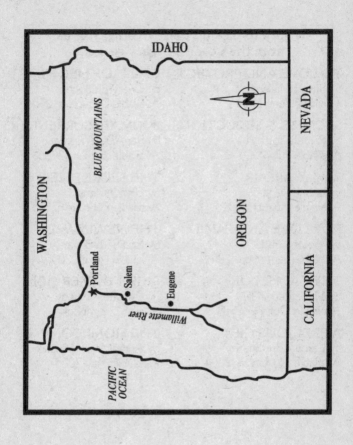

Be sure to pick up these riveting stories from the Logan's Legacy series:

One

"I don't have the time to explain it to you, mister. Eve Warwick—that's who I need. And come hell or high water, I'm going to see her and I'm going to see her now."

After a full ten minutes of going round and round with the Warwick butler, who was blocking the doorway of the sprawling Warwick family mansion, Hunter Coltrane had reached the limits of his patience. He had the man by the shirtfront, his face no more than an inch from the butler's nose.

Hunter could see that the much smaller man's features were tightened into a mask of abject fear. But at that moment the butler's fear was nothing compared to the fear Hunter felt, and he was too desperate to care that he was scaring the man. If scaring him was what it took, he'd terrify the guy.

"She's about to leave for an appointment and she'll fire me if I let you or anyone else delay her," the butler informed him in a strained whisper.

"Then how about if you don't *let* me delay her? How about if you just tell me where in this damn mausoleum she is and I go find her for myself?"

"What do you think you're doing?" a grating female voice demanded from inside the house just then.

Without breaking eye contact with the butler, Hunter recognized the speaker. That voice belonged to Eve Warwick. He ungently moved the other man out of his way, stepped across the threshold and went into the foyer of the imposing residence that he and his late wife had visited on only one occasion a little over four years ago.

Eve Warwick was standing at the top of a grand staircase that curved in a full half-circle sweep to the second level of the three-story structure. She looked as outraged as she sounded, but Hunter would suffer that outrage and anything else she wanted to dish out to get what he'd come for.

He consciously tried to calm the unusual flare of temper that frustration had raised and forced himself to speak civilly.

"I don't know if you remember me or not. I'm Hunter Coltrane," he said. "My wife and I adopted your baby—"

"I know who you are and you have no business here," Eve Warwick decreed imperiously.

"It isn't 'business' I'm here for. I'm here for Johnny. He's—"

"I don't care *what* you're here for. You just need to leave. Now," she ordered.

Hunter ignored it. "Johnny—that's what we named him—needs your blood," he informed her.

But not even blurting that out had an impact on the perfectly coiffed woman in the haute couture pink suit. Her only response was to transfer her gaze to the butler and say, "Pixley, call security."

"Just hear me out," Hunter implored. "Johnny is in the Portland General Hospital emergency room and he needs blood. *Your* blood. You know he has AB negative—your rare type. There was a bus accident yesterday and a whole family with that blood was hurt. They depleted all the blood bank had stored. But Johnny needs a transfusion in a hurry, so you have to come with me to the hospital. Right now!"

Hunter realized that his voice rang with his own worry for his son, but he didn't care.

"I did the open adoption through the Children's Connection to be sure the child went to the right people," Eve said. "*Not* so that I could be bothered by those people at any time afterward. If you'll recall, you signed an agreement to that effect. I'm sorry your son is ill, but it has nothing to do with me. So please leave."

She didn't sound sorry. She sounded cold, aloof and absolutely unconcerned.

"Did you not understand?" Hunter said, his voice raising an octave all on its own. "I'm not here to bother you and under any other circumstances I would have abided by that agreement and we wouldn't have ever seen each other again. But my son is in danger if he doesn't get the blood he needs. Immediately!"

Eve Warwick again turned a hard, demanding eye to the butler who was still standing where Hunter had left him. "Pixley?" she said snidely, "You can't call security as you were told to do if you're standing there eavesdropping."

"Yes, ma'am," the butler answered, pivoting on his heels and hurrying out of the foyer.

"Look," Hunter said, trying to reason with the woman. "I'm no happier to be here than you are to have me here. I guarantee that it was as much my goal as yours for us never to have contact again. But my son is in trouble and he needs your help. All you have to do is come with me to the hospital and give blood."

"I don't like needles," she said, raising her nose in the air. "And I have an appointment with my manicurist that I cannot miss. I'm sure you or the hospital will find someone else who can help. Portland, Oregon, is not the end of the earth, after all. There's bound to be someone else with AB negative blood."

"There isn't time to *find* someone else!" Hunter shouted, his frustration once again rearing its ugly head.

"There will have to be, because I'm not doing it, and that's all there is to it."

"That is *not* all there is to it," Hunter shouted so loudly his voice echoed in the marble-lined space and made the crystal chandelier overhead tinkle like a wind chime. "Whether you gave Johnny up or not, we're talking about your own flesh and blood! That has to mean *something* to you!"

"It means you're making me late for my appointment. That's the only thing it means to me. The child is yours. He's not my concern."

Hunter and his late wife had not thought highly of Eve Warwick when they'd met her for the interview after applying to adopt the infant she was to deliver three months later. She'd given the impression that the baby was just some sort of debris to be disposed of somehow. But he still couldn't believe what he was faced with at that moment. No matter how much money she and her entire family had, no matter how much social standing, no matter how glamorous the life she led, how could she possibly be denying blood to *any* child, let alone the child she'd given birth to?

"Please, just come with me to the hospital," Hunter said, thinking that if she wanted him to beg, he'd do it. He'd do anything for his son.

But it didn't matter. Still sounding like a spoiled child vetoing her nanny's suggestion of a bath, she said, "No."

"*No* is not an option," Hunter countered, heading for that oversized staircase, thinking that if he had to throw the woman over his shoulder and physically take her to the hospital, he'd do it, regardless of the consequences he might have to face later.

But he hadn't even made it to the first step when

two security guards rushed him. He got in a punch, but before he could do more than that, one of the guards yanked his arms behind his back to subdue him.

"Eve? What's going on?"

The female voice came from behind Hunter, at the front door, which had been left open after his unceremonious entrance.

He didn't recognize this voice, though. It was much more lilting and pleasant-sounding, in spite of the alarm it held.

"It's nothing, Terese," Eve Warwick said, as if the life crisis Hunter had just laid at her feet really wasn't worth the annoyance it was causing. "Nothing is going on."

"*Something* is going on," the other woman insisted as the butler returned to the foyer, and the security guard Hunter had hit shared the burden of restraining him.

The other woman came around Hunter then and he got a glimpse of her that confused him.

Unlike Eve Warwick, she wasn't wearing designer clothes. Instead she was dressed in a pair of jeans and a plain blouse with the sleeves of a sweater tied around her shoulders. Her burnished red hair was pulled back into a simple ponytail, and if she wore any makeup, it wasn't noticeable—all of which led Hunter to wonder if she was an employee, despite the fact that even the butler was more dressed up in his three-piece suit.

Yet the woman didn't show any signs of subservience as she stood in the center of the foyer surveying the situation and using a tone with Eve War-wick that was anything but obsequious or servile.

Her presence did prompt Eve to finally come down the stairs, however. As she did, she began to explain her version of what was going on. "This...*person* shoved Pixley out of the way and barged in. And I'm having him removed."

"How can you do this?" Hunter demanded through teeth clenched with rage.

"I can do anything I please," the haughty woman answered, barely sparing him a glance as if even that was beneath her.

The other woman paid him more attention, looking him straight in the eye when she said, "How can she do what?"

But before Hunter could answer her, the butler seemed to take some delight in doing that himself. "This man wants Miss Eve to go with him to the hospital to give blood for his son."

"The son she gave birth to," Hunter added pointedly, glaring at the heiress, who merely rolled her eyes in annoyance at that announcement.

But the jeans-clad woman didn't take that news in stride. "Eve's baby?" she said, as if everything had suddenly changed.

"He isn't a baby anymore. He's four and he's in trouble and he needs her blood," Hunter said, recapping once again for the benefit of the newcomer.

The fresh-faced woman stared at Eve. "Eve! You refused?"

"Oh, please, Terese, spare me. The man is over-wrought and—"

"Overwrought?" Hunter said sarcastically. "You bet I'm overwrought. My kid is lying in the emergency room and I'm here jumping through hoops for something that a phone call should have accomplished—if you had taken one of the six I made to you before I came over here!"

The woman Eve had referred to as Terese turned back to Hunter. Or, more precisely, to the security guards who held him captive.

"Let this man go," she ordered them.

"He was coming after me," Eve said petulantly.

"Well, he won't come after you now because I'm going to take care of this," the woman named Terese said. Then, to the security guards who were still holding Hunter, she said more firmly, "I mean it. Let him go."

Hunter was released after the second command, though the guards stayed within arm's reach.

"I'm Terese Warwick, Eve's twin sister," the woman introduced herself.

For a moment Hunter stared at her in surprise. There was a resemblance between the women, but not enough that he would have guessed they were twins.

"I know we don't look alike. We're fraternal twins," Terese Warwick said as if she knew what he was thinking.

"I'm Hunter Coltrane," he said, recovering from his shock. "My wife and I adopted your sister's baby."

"And he's in need of blood?"

"It's a freak thing. He took a little fall, nothing out of the ordinary. He was standing on a stool and it tipped over. But he hit his nose when he fell and it started to bleed. I did everything I could think of to stop it but when I couldn't, I took him to the emergency room. The doctors there couldn't get the bleeding to stop either. Now they're talking about hemophilia. But in the meantime, he's lost a lot of blood and he needs a transfusion, and your sister is the quickest hope for that."

"But you know how I am about needles, Terese," Eve said defensively, as if that were more an issue than a child's health.

"Sometimes, Eve, you amaze me," Terese said.

"Oh, I know, you're so much better, aren't you?" Eve countered contemptuously. "Why don't you just go do it then, Terese? If I looked like you do maybe I'd be a do-gooder, too. It *is* all you have going for you."

Terese didn't respond to that cutting comment. She returned her focus to Hunter as if it had never been said.

"It's okay," she told him. "I have the same blood type. I'll go with you to the hospital and do whatever you need."

"Come in," Terese called in answer to the knock on the hospital room door at nine o'clock that night.

After having given two pints of blood and staying

long enough for the doctors to make certain that her blood sugar level was back to normal and that she was able to stand without getting dizzy, she'd finally received the go-ahead to be released. So she was sitting in a chair, expecting her visitor to be a nurse with forms for her to sign.

But it wasn't a nurse whose head poked through the door. It was Hunter Coltrane.

"Are you decent?" he asked in the deepest, richest male voice she thought she'd ever heard.

"I never had to do anything but roll up my sleeve," she informed him with a laugh. A laugh that was almost giddy for no reason at all except that she'd spent the entire time since she'd met the man thinking about him. Wondering about him.

"Come in," she repeated, trying not to sound as eager as she felt. She told herself she wasn't necessarily eager to see Hunter Coltrane in particular, just that after so many hours in that room she was eager to see anyone.

Hunter accepted a second invitation, stepping inside and letting the door close behind him.

The room was small but none of the many doctors and nurses who'd come in and out of it had seemed to fill the space the way this man did. He was a commanding presence—over six feet tall, with broad, muscular shoulders and long, thick-thighed legs.

A nurse knocked and came in right behind him to tell Terese the release papers were being processed.

Apparently the nurse had also had contact with Hunter and Johnny because she was telling Hunter something about a milkshake that his son had liked.

The conversation didn't include Terese and while it went on she used the time to take a closer look at Hunter Coltrane.

She didn't know much about him except that he owned and ran a ranch outside of Portland—Eve had made a point of saying a ranch was a good place for a child to grow up. Now, looking at the man who had adopted her nephew, Terese couldn't help thinking that hard, outdoor work had served him well because he looked in robust health.

He was dressed for the part of a rancher, too. He had on cowboy boots, a denim shirt with the sleeves rolled up to his elbows, and jeans that were aged to a faded blue and fit him like an old friend. But it all worked for him better than the three-thousand-dollar suits her father had specially made in London. In fact, the rustic attire only contributed to the rugged good looks of a face that nature seemed to have taken pains to carve.

A face that was no longer as tense as it had been earlier.

A face that Terese studied now that he was standing there in front of her and she had the perfect opportunity.

He had a sharp, square jaw shadowed with a day's growth of dark beard that looked more sexy than unkempt, and a mouth that was not too full, not too thin. His eyes were the color of the topaz stone in a ring Terese had inherited from her grandmother—brown eyes shot through with brilliant specks of gold. His brow was square and unlined, and he wore his sun-streaked dark blond hair just a little full and disarrayed—not messy, but as if he'd run his hands through it more than once today and let it all fall naturally into slight waves. Certainly it was nothing at all like the no-hair-out-of-place men she encountered in the social circles she was accustomed to.

The nurse left them alone then and Hunter's attention returned to Terese. "How are you doing?" he asked, barely penetrating her preoccupation.

She consciously pulled herself out of that preoccupation and said, "I'm fine. I felt a little weak and light-headed for a while but they gave me juice and cookies and I'm okay now. They're letting me go home."

He pointed a thumb over his shoulder at the door the nurse had just gone through. "She'd told me before that you were getting out. That's why I'm here."

That sounded like it might evolve into a fast goodbye and Terese didn't want it to. Not before she knew how her nephew was. So she said, "More importantly, how is Johnny?"

If Hunter had been about to make a quick exit, it didn't show because he swung a leg over the wheeled stool the doctor had used and sat down across from her. "Johnny's okay," he announced with relief in his voice. "The nosebleed stopped. Finally. And the transfusion made him feel better. They're keeping him for forty-eight hours—something about checking his hemoglobin to make sure it stabilizes. But as long as he isn't bleeding, we're doing well."

"And during the forty-eight hours will they know if he has hemophilia or not?" The drive to the hospital had only taken about twenty minutes, but Hunter had filled her in on a few things along the way.

"Yeah, those results should be in before they let him go. They're pretty sure that's what we're dealing with, though. They said we'll have to be cautious but there's no reason to panic. It isn't a progressive disease or a debilitating one. Which is good."

"In other words, it's not something you'd want him to have, but it could be worse," Terese summarized.

"Right. I'm sorry you couldn't come in and see him. The nurses told me you wanted to, but between the nosebleed and the transfusion the poor kid was overwhelmed and not up for company."

"That's okay. I understand." But that didn't mean she hadn't been disappointed. She'd been hoping this would be an opportunity to meet her nephew. The nephew she probably wouldn't have any other chance to meet, even though it was something she'd always wanted.

"Once the bleeding stopped," Hunter was saying, "and the transfusion was over, Johnny was exhausted. He fell right to sleep."

Terese nodded. "I'm just glad he's okay."

"I'll be staying here with him but since he's out like a light now I thought I could run you home without him missing me."

"Your wife isn't here?" Terese asked, knowing that a married couple had adopted Eve's baby.

Hunter handsome features tensed again. "We lost her two years ago," he said quietly.

"Oh. I'm so sorry."

He didn't offer any more information on his wife's death and although Terese was curious, she didn't feel free to question him.

He continued with what he'd been saying before that. "I don't want you to have to take a cab home or bother anyone to pick you up."

"It's okay. I called the house when they told me I'd be able to leave and had a car sent to get me."

Did that sound pretentious? Terese hoped not. But just in case it did, she added, "I don't usually use the Town Cars or the drivers. I like driving myself. I have a small sedan. But since I rode here with you…"

It occurred to her that Hunter Coltrane was probably not interested in that many details of her means of transportation, so she stopped what she was saying and finished with, "But thanks for thinking of me."

The rancher's expression had relaxed once more and he laughed a wry laugh. "It's me who needs to be thanking you. I can't tell you how grateful I am that you came here and did this. I'm in your debt. If there's anything I can ever do to repay you…"

Terese didn't respond immediately to that. Ordinarily she would have merely waved away his appreciation and certainly she wouldn't have sought any kind of compensation.

But this wasn't an ordinary situation. And it struck her suddenly that even though she hadn't been allowed to meet her nephew today, his father's gratitude might be her chance—her *only* chance—to meet Johnny in the future.

"There is one thing I'd like," she said tentatively, nervous about doing what she was about to do, but afraid she'd regret it if she didn't.

"Anything," he said.

Terese felt sort of small for putting him on the spot, so before she told him what she wanted, she prefaced it. "Let me say up front that if it makes you uncomfortable you're free to refuse—absolutely free."

Terese could tell he was already slightly uncomfortable because he'd been sitting with his elbows on his wide-spread knees, leaning towards her, and now he sat up straight. But this was important to her so she soldiered on, although she couldn't keep herself from talking very fast.

"Here's the thing. For the three days after Johnny was born—and before you and your wife took custody—Eve didn't want anything to do with him. But I hated the thought that he was only being looked after by nurses so I spent a lot of time with him. I fed him and changed him and…" She was getting teary-eyed just remembering it. Remembering how much it had broken her heart when she'd had to accept that her sister really wasn't going to keep him.

"Anyway," she said, "I fell in love with him and then he was gone and… Well, I've always wished I'd been able to keep in touch with him. To know him and how he's doing. To watch him grow up, even from a distance…"

Hunter Coltrane's posture seemed more stiff than it had before and Terese rushed to ease whatever tension she might be raising in him. "There's no question in my mind that you're his parent, that you're his family. Please don't think I'd ever—*ever*—forget that. But I really would like to meet him. Totally on your terms," she was quick to add. "And he wouldn't have to know there's a connection if you don't want him to. You could just say I'm a friend, or the person who gave him blood, and leave it at that."

Now it was Hunter who didn't respond readily. Instead he seemed to be thinking it over. Or maybe he was just trying to come up with an excuse.

Worrying that she was out of line, she didn't wait for an answer and instead spoke again. "Honestly, don't feel obligated. I give blood regularly so if the blood bank's supplies hadn't been depleted Johnny might have gotten my blood, anyway, and I would never have known the difference. So if you want to keep everything the way it's been for the last four years, it's okay. It isn't as if I'll take the blood back or anything."

The joke was lame but she was trying to lighten the tone, to keep him from feeling pressured.

"Maybe it wouldn't even be what's best for Johnny," Terese continued, the words spilling out on their own at a breakneck pace before Hunter could respond even if he was ready to. "And I wouldn't do anything that wasn't good for him."

"It's okay," the rancher said then, holding up one hand, palm outward, to stop more of the verbal avalanche. "If you'd give me a minute I'd tell you that I don't see anything wrong with Johnny meeting you."

Despite the fact that she'd been hoping he would agree, she was shocked that he had.

"Really?" she said.

"Really."

"And you aren't saying that just because you feel as if you owe me anything? Because you don't. I wouldn't want to do anything that disturbs you. I know that sometimes an adoptive parent's security can be—"

"I'm not insecure about being Johnny's dad," Hunter assured her with a hint of a smile that let her know how true that was. "Adopted or not, he's my son and nothing is ever going to change that. I don't think I want him going over to your house or anything like that, but just to have you meet him? I don't see any problem with that."

Terese didn't want to tell him that her twin sister wouldn't want Johnny at the house any more than he did, so she merely agreed with his qualification. "No, I don't think it would be good for Johnny to be at the house either. I'd come to you. I could even do it here, while he's in the hospital, if you don't want me to know where you live or—"

"I'm not sure if seeing him in the hospital is a good idea. There are so many strangers and he's already pretty intimidated just by being here. But where we live isn't a secret."

"I'm willing to do it any way you want to do it," Terese said.

The rancher paused another moment, and she worried he might be having second thoughts. In fact, he paused for so long and seemed to be watching her so intently, that she began to think he was going to say no after all.

But then, as if he'd made some sort of decision, he said, "You know, I have a guest cabin at the ranch. Nothing fancy, but if you wanted to come out and spend a few days with us, you could meet Johnny and get to know him a little on his own territory. What would you say to that?"

She wasn't sure what to say to that, because she was so stunned that not only was he willing to let her meet her nephew, he was actually offering her a way to get to know the little boy. It was more than Terese had ever hoped for.

"That would be wonderful," she finally said.

"Can you take some time off work— *Do* you work?"

"I do. I teach psychology at Portland State University. But I'm on sabbatical right now so my time is my own."

"Great."

Another nurse knocked and opened the door just then, coming in with papers for Terese to sign.

Hunter stood to give the stool over to her. "I'll get out of the way so you can go home. But I'll call you as soon as I get Johnny out of here and we can set up a time for you to come to the ranch."

"I can't wait," Terese answered.

Hunter gave her a little wave then and left her to the nurse who showed her where to sign the release forms and then told her she was free to go.

"You'll probably want to put on that sweater," the nurse said as she left. "It's feeling very Octoberish out there tonight."

"Thanks, I'll do that."

Terese slipped the sweater over her head and then went to the small mirror on the wall to pull her shirt collar up and make sure she was presentable.

But as she smoothed her hair into place something else flashed through her mind—the image of Hunter Coltrane. The image of Hunter Coltrane with her.

"Now *that's* a pipe dream," she muttered to herself.

And no one knew it better than Terese.

Because Hunter Coltrane was handsome enough to stop traffic and she, as proven by the reflection in the mirror, was hardly the kind of woman who would so much as turn his head.

Her stepmother had always said it. So had Eve. Eve had alluded to it today. And it was an irrefutable fact—Terese Warwick was a Plain Jane.

The kind of Plain Jane who didn't attract even moderately attractive men on her own merits, let alone men like Hunter.

"And don't you forget it!" she commanded her reflection as if it were another person.

Then she left the hospital room, telling herself just to be glad she was going to get to meet her nephew.

She worked hard to erase the lingering mental image of her nephew's father, a mental image that had things inside her sitting up and taking notice.

Just the way the man himself had....

Two

"Uh, Johnny? What do we have going on there?"

It was Sunday evening and Hunter was expecting Terese to arrive at his ranch any minute. He'd had his son home from the hospital since Thursday and after some soul-searching, on Friday night he'd kept his word and called her to arrange a time for her to come out and stay so she could meet Johnny and get to know him.

She'd said she had charity functions to attend this weekend, so would it be all right if she got there around nine o'clock. Hunter had agreed. But she was late and since it was already past Johnny's bedtime, Hunter had gotten the boy ready for bed, complete with bath and pajamas. But the little boy had just dis-

appeared upstairs for a while and now that he'd returned to the living room, Hunter was surprised to see
the results of that trip.

"You look nice and I wanted to, too," Johnny informed him.

Leave it to his son to notice that he'd taken a second shower and shaved again today, and that he was
wearing slacks and a polo shirt rather than the jeans
and sweatshirt he would normally have been in on a
lazy Sunday evening.

"Come over here and let me see what you've done,"
Hunter said, trying not to laugh.

Johnny had just turned four last month and was
very intent on proving that he was more independent
than he had been before. But as Hunter sat on the coffee table and pulled his son to stand between his legs,
the boy seemed small and fragile to him.

"So what did you do to yourself?" Hunter asked,
surveying how his son had spruced himself up.

Johnny had flaming red hair that Hunter kept short
on the sides and in back. But he let the barber leave a
little on top and now Johnny had done something to
make only the front part stick straight up.

Hunter lightly patted the stiff-looking tips with his
palm. "How'd you do this?" he asked, careful to sound
impartial so as not to offend what his son was clearly
proud to have accomplished.

"My friend Mikey showed me. You wet your hair
and then you kinda comb it up with the bar of soap till
it stays. Then you let it get dry."

That was a relief. Hunter was afraid he'd used super-glue.

"It makes you cool," Johnny informed him.

"Cool," Hunter repeated. "Uh-huh."

Accepting the hairstyle for the moment, he lowered his gaze to his son's chubby-cheeked face with the sprinkling of freckles across his tiny nose.

"And did you wash your face again since your bath?" he asked, surprised since it was always a struggle to get his son to wash his face once, let alone twice.

"I din't wash it. I shaved just a little bit," Johnny informed him, rubbing a hand along his peach-skin jawline.

"You must have pressed kind of hard," Hunter observed. "Your cheeks are all red. You made sure you used the special razor I gave you, didn't you? It's more important than ever that you never touch mine, you know?"

"I know. 'Cuz yours has a really sharp thing in it and 'cuz of the hemolilia I got now."

Hunter had tried to get him to pronounce hemophilia correctly but it was a losing battle.

"Right. And did you put some of the soap in your eyebrows to make them stand up, too?" Hunter asked, seeing that the pale brows over his son's blueberries-and-cream colored eyes were going in all directions.

"No, I think they musta just getted that way when I dried off my face 'cuz the water in my hair dripped."

"So can I fix them?"

Johnny nodded and Hunter licked his thumbs and smoothed his son's eyebrows into place.

Then he glanced down at Johnny's rodeo pajamas. And the way his son had accessorized them.

"That's one of my best ties, isn't it?"

"Yup. I wanted to look nice."

"And you do," Hunter assured him. He couldn't stop the smile that escaped. The tie was knotted into a wad at his throat and hung nearly to his knees. "I'm just thinking that this might not be a necktie kind of night. See? I don't have one on."

"Maybe you should put one on."

"I don't think so. And you know, a tie is sort of fancy for pajamas. Even for the good rodeo pajamas."

"I look nice," Johnny insisted.

"You do. You do. I'm just thinking that our company might not have dressed up quite that much and we wouldn't want her to feel bad, would we?"

Johnny creased his forehead and looked down at the striped tie. "We could tell her it was okay that she didn't get dressed up good as us."

"You really want to leave the tie on, huh?"

"Yup."

Hunter nodded. He didn't have the heart to force the issue. "Okay, then. Well, I guess since you're all ready, you can help me get the rest of your toys put away so this place doesn't look like a cyclone hit it."

Apparently feeling dressed up made the little boy agreeable because he didn't balk at that suggestion the way he usually did. Instead he turned and went right to work.

"Who's this lady again?" Johnny asked as he picked up his toys.

Hunter hadn't known how to explain Terese Warwick. Johnny knew he was adopted; Hunter and his wife had decided when he was still an infant that they would be open and honest with him on the subject. Despite that, the whole concept seemed slightly out of his grasp yet. Whenever they talked about it Johnny seemed only concerned with the fact that Hunter was his dad no matter what.

Hunter hadn't wanted to confuse him by trying to explain that Terese Warwick was the sister of Johnny's birth mother, so he'd opted for a more simple description. Which he repeated now.

"She's a friend who knew you when you were only a baby, and she's the person who has the same kind of blood that you have, so she gave you some of hers when you were in the hospital."

"When I was bleedin' on accounta the hemolilia."

"When your nose was bleeding so badly because of the hemophilia, yes."

"Is she your girlfriend like Mindy Harper wants to be my girlfriend and kiss me?" Johnny asked, being silly.

"When did Mindy Harper want to kiss you?"

"Before last week. At preschool. When we were havin' graham crackers and yogurt. She told Mikey she loooved me and she wanted to kiss me and I said yuk."

Again Hunter suppressed a smile. "No, the lady

who's coming to stay with us for a while is not my girlfriend and there won't be any kissing going on. She's
just a friend who's a girl. And really she'll be here to
see you more than to see me."

"Oh, no!" Johnny shouted in a panic.

It was an indication of how on-edge Hunter still was
about his son and his son's health that that simple ex-
clamation was enough to tense his entire body and
make him spin around to face the boy.

But Johnny's current crisis was far less distressing
than the one the week before.

"I forgetted about my hair and put my hat on!" the
little boy informed him, holding up his cowboy hat. "I
gotta fix it!" Then he dashed back upstairs.

"Don't put any more soap in it," Hunter called after
him. "Just use a little water if you have to."

Hunter shook his head and laughed to himself at his
son's antics. Then he returned to straightening up the
living room.

He knew that it wasn't Terese Warwick herself that
had Johnny so excited. The little boy didn't know her,
after all. It was merely the novelty of having someone
come to stay with them.

Hunter, on the other hand, was a different story. For
him it was the woman he was looking forward to seeing again. And he was none too happy about it.

In fact, wanting to see her again was what had
caused him to drag his feet about calling her to arrange
this visit.

Wanting to see any woman hadn't happened to him

since Margee. It sure as hell hadn't happened to him since Margee's death.

But with Terese Warwick it had happened. And it had Hunter feeling pretty unsettled. And confused. Why her, of all people? he kept asking himself.

Of course, she didn't seem anything like her sister. But maybe the difference between them was actually the problem.

For all her money and high-class social circles, Terese still had a sort of girl-next-door thing going for her. And flashy, overly made-up, beauty-shop-perfect women—like Eve Warwick—put him off. Who wanted somebody who looked as if they needed to be kept on a pedestal and dusted once a week? Somebody who might as well have a hands-off sign posted on her forehead?

But the girl-next-door thing? That had more appeal to him. Give him Terese's long, thick ponytail over her sister's helmet hair any day. That ponytail was the color of red oak and shiny and neat and clean.

Give him those few freckles that dotted Terese's pale porcelain skin, keeping her from being too perfect and putting a hint of mischief into her appearance. And there was no doubt that he preferred Terese's pert nose to that surgeon-fashioned one her sister sported.

Plus, Terese's eyes didn't need all that glitter and fake stuff on the lids, he thought as he tossed a few more of his son's toys into one of the cupboards that lined a wall of the living room. Terese had eyes that were incredible on their own. Warm, sparkling, iridescent, vibrant blue eyes, with lustrous dark lashes. He'd rather be looking into those eyes any day of the week than into those cold baby-blues of her sister.

Oh yeah, given a choice, he'd vote for the natural, fresh-scrubbed beauty. And when it came attached to a tight little body with breasts that were just the right size…

"Geez," he muttered to himself in disgust, knowing he didn't have any business thinking about her breasts. Not now and not the other ten dozen times he had in the last several days.

It was just that something about Terese had gotten to him.

But it wasn't only the way she looked that kept coming back into his head to taunt him. Or the way she looked that seemed to set her apart from her twin sister. Terese also seemed sweet and kind and unselfish, though not in a doormat sort of way. After all, she'd stood her ground with her nasty sister and that was saying something.

But at the same time, Terese's sweetness and kindness and unselfishness had seemed natural, too. Innate. And bolstered by a strength of character her twin clearly lacked.

And so there he was, Hunter thought as he jammed more toys into the cupboard and had to force the door closed. He'd taken two showers in one day, he'd gotten himself dressed up, and he was having problems holding down his own excitement at the prospect of Terese Warwick arriving on his doorstep any minute now.

Excitement he was none too happy about at the moment.

All it did was get him riled up for no good reason.

And why?

Because of the who and the when.

The who being that she was Terese Warwick. Which meant that no matter how much appeal she might have, it came in the shadow of her sister and the fact that her sister was Johnny's birth mother.

And if that shadow wasn't enough, Hunter also knew he needed to keep uppermost in his mind the fact that though Terese seemed like the girl-next-door, she wasn't. She was someone who operated on a whole different level than he did. She was someone who lived in a whole different world than he did.

Oh yeah, *who* she was was sure as hell something he needed to keep in mind.

And as for the *when* part?

The when part was even more important. So important that if Terese Warwick wasn't a Warwick at all, if she was the most amazing, beautiful, perfect, wonderful woman on the face of the earth, he still wouldn't do anything about it.

Because right now was not the time for a woman in his life. For any woman. Right now was Johnny's time.

It was a vow Hunter had made to himself. Johnny

was his priority. Johnny was the one and only person he was devoted to.

Maybe not forever, because he knew that eventually his son would be more interested in his own friends and activities and wouldn't want his old Dad hanging around. But for now, for as long as dad was the center of Johnny's universe, Hunter wouldn't take that lightly. He wouldn't let there be any distractions, any intrusions. Not by anyone.

So Terese Warwick couldn't have more than a superficial place in their lives and that was all there was to it.

Which was why he had no business looking forward to her coming. No business getting excited.

But whether he had any business doing all that or not, the feeling was there, anyway.

So he guessed he'd just have to keep it under wraps. Keep it from flourishing. And he'd also have to make sure he didn't let anything come of any of it.

This was going to be Johnny's time with Terese, and her time with him. Hunter would just stand on the sidelines and oversee it. He'd keep himself as removed from it as he could.

That was his plan.

But damn if he wouldn't feel a lot better if this excitement would go away and leave him in peace.

It was almost nine-thirty when Terese finally found the wooden arch that proclaimed Hunter Coltrane's ranch, the Double Bar S, and turned from the main road onto the gravel drive.

The drive was lined on both sides by a white rail fence that bordered grassy fields where several cows grazed lazily and watched her without enthusiasm. It was a sentiment she hoped Hunter Coltrane didn't share at the prospect of having her there.

She was surprised by how small the house was when it came into view in the distance. Of course, not only was the white two-story farmhouse in the midst of a vast expanse of open ground, there were also an enormous white barn and a silo looming up behind it, and it occurred to her that they might be dwarfing Hunter's home, too.

It was a well-kept little house, though, with black shutters neatly decorating each window. The first level was larger than the second and there was a big covered front porch with a crossbuck railing around it that gave the place an inviting, homey feel.

Terese pulled to a stop at the end of the drive where there was a patch of manicured lawn and a cobbled sidewalk led the rest of the way to the house.

Stretching along the porch were brick-bordered flower beds. Although it was too late in the year for blooms, the flower beds were festively adorned with teepees of dried corn stalks and artfully displayed pumpkins, brightly colored gourds and squashes. There was also a life-sized stuffed scarecrow dressed in a red bandana shirt and denim overalls lounging on the chair swing that hung from chains at one end of the porch.

All in all, even though the place was nothing fancy, Terese liked it.

A porch light to the right of the screened front door was lit for her, providing a warm golden glow even after she'd turned off her engine and her car lights. She got out from behind the wheel and just stood there for a moment, looking at the house and letting it sink in that her nephew really was just inside.

In those first few days of his life, she'd fallen in love with the baby Eve had given birth to. She'd held him and rocked him and cooed to him. She'd felt him curl up against her; she'd spent hours with him sleeping in her arms.

In the process she'd begun to hope that her sister would change her mind about giving up the baby. That she could convince her sister to keep him and that then she would get to be a part of his life.

But nothing she'd said or done had changed Eve's mind. Eve had wanted nothing to do with that baby. She didn't want to see him. She didn't want to hold him. She didn't even want to know he was alive. And she certainly wasn't going to keep him.

When Terese had finally had to accept that, her thoughts had turned to an alternate course. She'd decided to adopt the baby herself.

Eve had hit the ceiling when Terese had told her. It was the biggest argument they'd ever had, culminating in Eve's flat refusal to relinquish the infant to Terese. Then, to make it even harder on Terese, Eve had arranged for the baby to be immediately turned over to the parents Eve had chosen. Terese hadn't had so much as the opportunity to say goodbye to the baby she'd come to love.

It had wrenched Terese's heart. In fact, she'd gone through a long period of grieving before she'd given up the hope of ever seeing him again.

And then she'd come home to find Hunter Coltrane in her entryway.

Of course the circumstances had been less than ideal. Certainly she didn't want a health problem to be the cause of bringing her nephew back into her life. But now that it had happened and she was only moments away from getting to see him again, it seemed too good to be true.

Terese opened the rear door and pulled out her leather suitcase, not wanting to waste any more precious time when she could be meeting her nephew.

And seeing his dad again.

But Terese pushed the thought of Hunter out of her mind as soon as it popped into it. Exactly as she'd been doing since she'd seen him at the hospital. Hunter might be drop-dead gorgeous and honest enough to have kept his word, but meeting and getting to know his son was the only thing this visit was about. And she couldn't let herself forget that.

Terese was determined not to lose sight of just how touchy the whole situation was. She knew she had to keep in mind that she was an outsider in the lives of both father and son. She had to keep in mind that even though she might be a blood relative of Johnny's, she still had no rights to him, that she was nothing more than a stranger here, allowed to get to know him only out of the kindness and generosity of his father, a father who could very well have dug in his heels and refused to have the line between birth family and adopted family crossed.

No, she had no doubt whatsoever that this was a touchy situation. Touchy and complicated. And it didn't need to be complicated even more by her drifting into thoughts of Hunter Coltrane as a man.

Terese closed the rear car door with a resounding slam, as if that would help put an end to any thoughts of her nephew's father.

Then she climbed the four steps to the front porch with her suitcase in hand.

But before she had a chance to knock on the screen, the carved oak door opened and there stood Hunter Coltrane.

Tall. Broad-shouldered. Strappingly good-looking.

Taller, broader of shoulder, and even more strappingly good-looking than her memory had made him in all the images that had haunted her since she'd come in on his confrontation with her sister this past week.

It didn't help matters.

But Terese tamped down the instant, involuntary appreciation that flooded her at that first sight of him and reminded herself that she was out of his league when it came to looks, and that she'd better remember it.

Johnny. This was only about Johnny....

"I'm sorry I'm late," she said in lieu of a greeting

as he pushed open the screen. "I'm the chairwoman for the committee that gave this dinner tonight and I just couldn't seem to get away."

"It's okay. The man of the hour is still awake and champing at the bit to meet you," the rancher said in that lush, masculine voice she'd been hearing call her name in her dreams.

As if on cue, a little boy bounded down the stairs behind Hunter just then, shouting as he did, "Is she here? Is she here?"

"What'd I tell you about comin' down those steps more slowly and holdin' on to the railing so you don't fall, little man?" Hunter asked sternly.

"I know," the small boy grumbled half under his breath. "But is she here?"

Hunter still didn't answer that. He turned back to Terese, propped the screen open with his backside and reached for her suitcase.

"I hope you're ready for this," he said. "Come on in."

"Thanks," Terese muttered as she crossed the threshold in front of him, catching a whiff of a light, heady aftershave that smelled like a pine forest.

The big man had been blocking a clear view of the little boy but once she'd stepped into the entryway Johnny was right there, in full sight, fidgeting with excitement.

"I'm Johnny!" the pajama and necktie-clad child proclaimed proudly.

Terese had no idea how his father had explained her

so, as she drank in that first opportunity to set eyes on him in four years, she simply said, "Hi, Johnny. I'm Terese." But there was a catch in her throat as a combination of emotions put moisture in her eyes and made her smile too big at the same time.

There he is, she just kept thinking as he held out a tiny hand for her to shake as if she were a visiting dignitary.

He couldn't have been more adorable with that chubby-cheeked, freckled face, that turned-up nose and that fiery red hair that he'd done something with to make it stand at attention in front. And in that instant, Terese fell in love with him all over again.

She wanted badly to scoop him up and hug him, but of course she didn't do that for fear of frightening him. She did probably hold on to his hand a shade longer than she should have.

"Nice to meet you, Johnny," she said, finally letting go of him.

"What's our deal?" Hunter asked then.

Terese glanced over her shoulder at him to see whom he was talking to and found him leaning a shoulder against the door he'd just closed, his thumbs hooked in the pockets of his slacks, observing this meeting.

His question had been aimed at his son, though, and Johnny knew it because the little boy said, "I can show her 'round the house and have one short story and then I have to go to sleep." It had been a recitation peppered with reluctance and it made Terese smile all over again. Especially when Johnny added, "Can our company read me the story?"

"Our *company's* name is Miss Warwick."

"Oh, no, please, I'm Terese," she implored.

"Okay. It's up to Terese whether or not she wants to read you a story. Maybe she'd rather get settled in," Hunter told his son.

"I'd love to read the story," Terese interjected.

"She'd love to read the story," Johnny repeated for his father, making Hunter chuckle.

He raised his sculpted chin in the general direction of the house then. "Okay. Well, get to it, Mr. Tour Guide."

A tour guide was exactly the persona the small child put on for her as he led Terese from the entryway to the living room that opened to the right.

"This is where we play games and watch TV," Johnny said as if Terese wouldn't know what the room was used for otherwise. "There's not s'posed to be food in here since I spilled the orange juice on the couch and we had to turn over the pillow so nobody'd know."

"Johnny…" Hunter groaned from behind them.

But Terese merely laughed again—both at the son giving away secrets and the father's embarrassment. "You would never know by looking," she assured, glancing at the gray tweed sofa that matched an overstuffed easy chair.

They were positioned with an oak coffee table and a full wall of shelves and cabinets that, from what she could see, acted as an entertainment center, library and knickknack holder in front of them. Solid wood doors blocked the view of the contents of the lower cabinets.

"The kitchen's this way," Johnny said, heading through an open arch to the right of the living room.

It was a big country kitchen with an abundance of plain white cupboards and appliances and a large pedestal table with four barrel-backed chairs around it.

"This is where we eat—even at Christmas and stuff. My friend Mikey's got another room where they eat on Christmas but we don't."

"That means there's no formal dining room," Hunter translated from where he'd stopped in the kitchen's entrance.

"Ah," Terese said.

"This is the mudroom," Johnny informed her, pointing into the much smaller space that was off the kitchen. It contained a washer and dryer as well as a shelf with coat hooks and a bench beneath it. "My dad says it was named for me because I'm always comin' in muddy and I need to take off my shoes in there before I track it everywhere else."

"Good idea," Terese confirmed.

"So if you get muddy feet, you can do that, too."

"I'll remember that."

"Now we can go upstairs," Johnny announced.

Terese followed him back into the living room, casting Hunter a faint smile when she glanced back to see if he was coming, too.

But he didn't catch the smile because his eyes were too low. In fact, she thought they might have been on her rear end.

Had Hunter Coltrane been checking out her derriere?

She must have been mistaken, she told herself. But even so, she couldn't help the little rush that went through her.

A little rush she tried to ignore.

They returned to the stairs Johnny had run down earlier and went up to the second floor.

"That's the bathroom over there. Always knock first," Johnny said, adding his advice by rote. Next he held one arm straight out and pointed a miniature index finger at another door. "That's the guest bedroom for when somebody has a sleepover but doesn't stay in the cabin." The index finger moved slightly. "That's my dad's room." Another move of the index finger. "And this one is mine!"

Terese couldn't see into the guest bedroom because the door was closed, but she did catch a glimpse of a tall antique bureau and a king-size bed with a fluffy brown comforter in the room Johnny had said belonged to his father.

There was no time for more than that glimpse, though, as her nephew charged into his own room, clearly intending her to go with him.

"Come on, I'll get the book for you to read."

Terese went into the toy-cluttered room, but as she did, she once more cast a glance to Hunter. "You're sure you don't mind my doing the honors?" she asked, wanting to make sure she wasn't stepping on any toes.

"It's okay," Hunter assured, leaning a single shoulder against the doorframe and crossing his arms over his chest. He didn't say any more to Terese but aimed his attention at his son once again. "The necktie has to come off for bed."

The little boy obeyed without an argument, brought the tie to his father and then situated himself to one side of the bed so Terese could sit on the mattress beside him.

"Green Eggs and Ham," Johnny said when he handed the chosen book to her. "My dad is tired of it but maybe you're not."

"I don't think I've ever read *Green Eggs and Ham,* so it will be a treat for me."

Reading to him *was* a treat for her, but the book itself had little to do with it. Just the fact that Terese was sitting there with her nephew, participating in his bedtime routine, was something more special to her than either Johnny or his father could know.

She was sorry when she reached the last page.

As she closed the book, the little boy slid under the covers and said, "You'll be here tomorrow, right?"

"I will be," Terese confirmed.

"We gots ranch work to do but I'm gonna show you our barn and our barn cat and all the stuff outside that I couldn't show you in the dark."

"I'd like that."

She also would have liked to bend over and give

him a good-night kiss on the cheek or the forehead, but, as with the urge to hug him earlier, she resisted. Instead she said, "I'll see you in the morning, then," and traded places with Hunter to stand at the doorway while he tucked Johnny in, roughed up his hair and gave him the good-night kiss she hadn't been able to.

"Sleep tight, big guy," Hunter said once the ritual was accomplished.

"Sleep tight," Johnny answered, already sounding groggy.

Hunter switched on a small bedside lamp and then joined Terese at the door, turning off the overhead light.

She stepped aside to allow him to go out into the hall but once he had she couldn't keep herself from craning around the doorjamb for one more look at her nephew.

A wealth of emotions swelled in her and she had an odd feeling that he might once again disappear from her life if she left him behind.

But of course that was silly. She knew she was going to see the little boy again the next day. Reminding herself of that finally made her able to tear herself away from the door.

Once she had, Hunter motioned toward the stairs without saying anything and waited for Terese to precede him.

Not until they were at the foot of the steps did he say, "So that's our boy."

Our boy. That pleased Terese. "I wasn't sure if he

knew exactly who I was," she said then, recalling her introduction to her nephew.

"I didn't go into the details," Hunter answered, explaining what he had told Johnny about her.

She didn't mind her nephew thinking of her as only a friend of the family so as not to confuse him and she let his father know that.

"This way," Hunter said in conclusion, "he's just happy to have company."

There didn't seem to be any more to say on that subject so Terese felt free to voice the other question she'd been anxious to ask. "What about the blood test? Does he have hemophilia?"

Hunter nodded. "'Fraid so. But now that we know, we can deal with it."

"Which is why you didn't want him running down the stairs," Terese guessed.

"Mmm. I'm probably being overly cautious right now because this episode last week kind of shook me, but yes, he needs to be more careful than most kids since it's so easy for the bleeding to get out of control if he's hurt."

"Well, at least now you know where you can get him a refill," Terese joked.

Hunter had been very quiet since her arrival but that comment garnered her a smile. A warm smile that softened his features and made her stomach flutter.

Hunter seemed to realize they were still standing at the foot of the steps and nodded in the direction of the kitchen. "Can I get you something to eat or drink? Or shall I just show you the cabin?"

It hadn't struck Terese until then that Hunter was

hanging back, making her visit only for his son and not participating any more himself than was absolutely necessary. Now that she realized it, she figured he'd prefer showing her where she'd be staying rather than having to socialize with her.

Which was probably how it should have been anyway, she told herself through the wave of disappointment she knew was totally inappropriate.

So, again thinking to give him what she assumed he wanted, she said, "I'm fine. I mean I don't need anything to eat or drink. You can just show me the cabin."

He didn't argue. He just picked up her suitcase and led her out the back door.

Terese paused a moment to look around when she got outside. An industrial-sized light on the barn illuminated the entire area.

The grounds were divided into the plain dirt patch and fenced-in paddock that were immediately in front and to the side of the barn, and a small, grassy yard like any suburban backyard. There was a jungle gym waiting to be played on beneath a tall oak tree, a brick patio complete with a barbecue, several trucks and toys here and there, and, about eight or nine feet off the south side of the house, there was, indeed, a log cabin.

"The cabin was the first house here," Hunter informed her as he led her down the brick path that connected it to what was now the main house. "My great-great-great-grandfather built it when he bought the land and he and my great-great-great-grandmother and their three kids lived in it their whole lives. There've been a few amenities added over the years—you have heat and electricity and plumbing now—but most of it is original and rustic. Nothing like what you're used to, I'm afraid."

The door was unlocked when they reached the cabin and Hunter opened it and flipped a switch that flooded the space with light. Then he waited for Terese to go in ahead of him and followed her in just enough to set her suitcase down.

He hadn't been joking about it being rustic. The walls were log and mortar and it was a single open space that, while not cramped for one person, was impossible to imagine for five.

But there was a four-poster double bed, a dresser, an easy chair and a television, a café-sized table with two chairs, and a black woodburning stove that had probably been the only source of heat for the place originally.

"It's rustic but nice," Terese said, meaning it.

"The bathroom is through that door over there," he said then, pointing it out. "There are some mugs and tea bags and cocoa and instant coffee. You can heat water in that microwave over there if you want any of that. But there's no kitchen otherwise. I leave the mudroom door open, though, so you can raid the fridge even in the middle of the night if you get hungry. Otherwise, we'll be eatin' regular meals together."

"I don't usually raid the refrigerator at night, anyway."

"Wish I could say the same thing. Anyway, we usually have breakfast around eight but I'll be up and about doin' chores long before that, so if you hear anything, don't think there are burglars or something, and don't feel as if you can't stay in bed a while longer. I'm usually up before dawn but Johnny'll be sleepin' later than that."

"Before dawn? Really?"

"Rancher's hours. It isn't so bad. You get used to it," he said. "So, anything else I can do for you or get you?"

"Nothing I can think of."

"All right, then." Hunter took two steps to get back out the door and Terese went to the threshold behind him.

"I want you to know how grateful I am for this," she said, not wanting him to get away without telling him that. "When I didn't hear from you until Friday, I thought you might have had second thoughts."

"I did do some thinking before I made the call," he admitted with a half smile that was a little guilty and only more charming because of it.

"But you let me come, anyway," Terese said, wondering where the almost flirtatious tone had come from when she hadn't intended it.

"I think it'll be okay."

"I'll do my best to make it okay. I know this can't be something you've dreamed of."

"Don't be too sure of that," he said more to himself than to her.

Terese had no idea what that meant and didn't feel as if she could question him about it. And since he didn't offer an explanation, she continued with what she'd wanted to say. "I'll be really careful not to over-step my bounds. I don't have any illusions about being a part of your family and I know Johnny is your son."

"I appreciate that," Hunter said, his topaz eyes meeting hers.

"He seems like a great kid, though," she said then.

"He is a great kid. But a pistol, in case you missed that."

"I didn't," Terese said with a laugh. "It's part of what I liked."

"Me, too," Hunter confided.

Something about that confidence gave Terese a sense that that hanging back he'd been doing was over, that they'd just shared something that broke down a wall of some kind. And she was glad.

Even though, as a result, her mind started to wan-der in a direction all its own and she began to compare this moment with Hunter at the door to the end of a date.

"I guess I'll see you tomorrow morning for break-fast, then," he said after a moment.

"I expect to do my share so don't think you need to cook for me or anything," Terese said.

"I'll be cookin' one way or another. But maybe you could take a turn of your own," he suggested with a hint of mischief to his tone.

Terese guessed what was on his mind. "You think I can't, don't you?"

He shrugged one broad shoulder and arched a challenging eyebrow at her. "Can you?"

"Maybe you'll just have to wait and see."

Oh, more of the flirting. What was she doing?

"Maybe I'll just have to," he countered. And unless she was mistaken, there was a hint of flirtatiousness in his voice, too.

But then he seemed to catch himself because he drew back almost imperceptibly and took another step away from the cabin door.

"I'll let you get settled in," he said.

Terese nodded. "Good night."

"'Night," he answered, turning on his heels and heading for the house.

But even though that hanging-back thing he'd been doing earlier had returned at the last minute, Terese was still fighting those images of this as the end of a date.

The end of a date when a kiss might have been possible...

A kiss from Hunter?

Even thinking about that was out of those bounds she'd just told him she would stay in.

But out of bounds or not, that was exactly what she was thinking about as she finally closed the cabin door.

Three

The next morning at eight o'clock on the dot Terese left the cabin. She'd been up for more than an hour by then, showered, shampooed her hair and braided it into a thick plait down her back. She'd dressed in one of the three pairs of jeans she'd bought for this visit—not the trouser-cut jeans she ordinarily wore, but the five-pocket kind—and a red turtleneck, also purchased when she'd shopped cluelessly for what to wear on a ranch.

She'd debated about going over to the house before eight to see if she could help prepare breakfast. But since her host had said eight, she'd thought that maybe he hadn't wanted her there before that and had refrained. That didn't change the fact that she was eager to get back to Johnny. And Hunter—although she really, really tried to keep the Hunter part of that at bay.

It was just that her mind kept replaying the end of last evening, and every time it did, eagerness to see him again slipped under her radar.

So as she walked along the brick path to the house, she once more reminded herself that this visit was about the opportunity for her to connect with Johnny. Hunter was nothing more than incidental to that goal.

Incidental or not, when Terese knocked on the mud-room door and a woman her own age opened it, a pang of something very unpleasant shot through her.

"You must be Terese," the woman said warmly, pushing open the screen as if she were letting Terese into her own home. "I'm Carla."

Carla.

Who was Carla?

"Hi," Terese said, stepping inside as the wheels of her mind began to spin with questions not only about Carla's identity, but whether she had been the reason Hunter had seemed eager to end the previous evening as soon as Johnny was in bed. Had Carla been due to come over afterward and spend the night?

Terese told herself that none of that was her business. Hunter Coltrane was a grown man—an amazingly handsome, masculine, sexy and no doubt virile grown man—and there was no reason he couldn't or shouldn't have female companionship. He was, after all, single and available.

She also told herself that there was no reason for

her to feel so awkward suddenly about being there herself because nothing about her visit had changed just because there was now a Carla.

But she felt terribly awkward, anyway.

"'Mornin'," Hunter called from the kitchen.

Terese would have liked to turn tail and run back to the cabin to hide until she could regain her equilibrium. Unable to do that, she forced a cheery face and followed Carla into the kitchen.

"Good morning," she said, answering Hunter's greeting and wishing she could blend into the wallpaper.

"You don't ever have to knock, you know," he informed her. "Just go ahead and let yourself in. Anytime."

Terese nodded, looking around the big country kitchen for Johnny. But he wasn't there. It was only Hunter setting three places at the table and Carla, who had moved to the coffeepot.

"Can I get you a cup?" the other woman asked Terese, again as if she were right at home.

"Yes. Thank you," Terese answered somewhat stiffly, taking in the sight of the pretty brunette with the dark eyes and flawless skin and a bust size Terese couldn't even come close to measuring up to.

"How'd you sleep?" Hunter asked her then, apparently feeling no inclination to explain Carla's presence.

The first thing that popped into Terese's mind was that she'd probably gotten a whole lot more sleep than these two had. But all she said was, "Fine. That's the most comfortable bed I've ever slept in."

"Glad to hear it," Hunter said.

"Where's Johnny?" she asked then, hoping she would feel less like a third wheel if her nephew would appear.

It was Carla who answered her question, though, by hollering for the boy as if it were something she did regularly. Then, handing Terese a mug of steaming coffee, she said, "He'll be right down. Sugar and cream are over there."

This was silly, Terese lectured herself as she took her coffee cup to the kitchen table that Hunter had set and had now left to go to the stove. She hadn't come here with designs on Hunter Coltrane. She hadn't come here with any illusions that they would form any kind of relationship that didn't revolve solely around Johnny. So what if Hunter had a girlfriend or a significant other or whatever Carla was? Why should it make her feel so uncomfortable? So weird? So...

Jealous? Was she feeling jealous? That couldn't be....

The mud room door opened again just then and Terese turned in that direction, wondering why Carla had aimed for the upstairs when she'd called Johnny if the little boy was coming in from outside somewhere.

But it wasn't Johnny who joined them a moment later. It was a tall man with coal-black hair and a bushy mustache.

"Where's my coffee, woman?" he demanded play-fully of Carla, wrapping an arm around her waist and pulling her up against his side.

"I'm pouring it right now. Behave yourself," Carla chastised, nodding toward Terese before she said, "This is Terese. Terese, this is my Willy."

"Willy works the ranch with me," Hunter explained then. "Carla comes over when she has a little time on her hands and helps out with things around the house."

Never had Terese felt the kind of relief she did at that moment.

"It's nice to meet you, Willy," she said, her cheeri-ness genuine this time. And probably out of propor-tion to the simple introduction of the ranch hand.

"John Paul Coltrane, get yourself down here now," Hunter called in a booming voice as he set a platter laden with scrambled eggs, bacon and sausages on the table.

"He's doing something with his hair to look nice for Terese," Carla confided.

Hunter grimaced. "Not that slicking up the front with soap again?"

"I think so."

"He did that last night, too."

"Well, I'm going up to clean the bathroom and I'll send him down," Carla said. Then, as she headed out of the kitchen, she added, "If I don't see you again be-fore I leave, Terese, it was nice meeting you."

"You, too," Terese said with more enthusiasm now that she knew the other woman wasn't Hunter's girl-friend.

"I'm headin' out again, too. I'll take this coffee to the barn with me," Willy added, retracing his steps through the mudroom.

And suddenly the whirlwind that Terese had walked in on had passed and she was alone with Hunter.

And much happier than she'd been moments earlier.

Of course Hunter was oblivious to the turmoil she'd just induced in herself, and he merely motioned toward one of the barrel-backed chairs for her to sit down.

"We might as well get started before everything's cold," he said, not taking the chair across from her until she was seated.

Terese had been so enmeshed in imagining a romance between Hunter and Carla that she hadn't taken much of a look at Hunter before. But now she did, surreptitiously making note that ranch-wear was pointy-toed cowboy boots, jeans that fitted him to perfection, and a chambray shirt with the sleeves rolled up to just below his elbows, exposing muscular forearms and wrists that seemed sexier than mere forearms and wrists could possibly be.

"So Willy and Carla are married?" Terese heard herself say without considering—until after the fact—whether she was being nosy.

But if Hunter thought she was, he didn't seem to take offense. He just answered her question. "They've been married for a long time now. Since we all graduated from high school." He handed her the platter of food and then added, "I was best man at their wedding and they were best man and matron of honor at mine."

"You must be very good friends," Terese said as she took some of the eggs and a piece of bacon.

"Willy's more than a good friend," Hunter amended, putting some of everything on Johnny's plate and then serving himself. "Will's closer to me than my brother. We work together every day. Spend time together when we aren't workin'. We own a boat together. We fish and hunt and watch every football game together. He's Johnny's godfather. I'd give him the shirt off my back if he needed it, and I know he'd do the same for me. And Carla… Well, Carla was my wife's best friend and she's Johnny's godmother. I don't think Johnny or I could have made it through the last two years without them both."

Which left Terese feeling all the more ridiculous for the conclusion she'd jumped to about the woman and her relationship with Hunter.

What had gotten into her? she asked herself.

But she decided it was some kind of fluke that would never happen again and that it was best to put it behind her.

"I've never had friends like that," she admitted then. "I couldn't even say any of that about Eve."

"I don't think many people are lucky enough to have friends like Will and Carla."

Johnny came running into the kitchen then, putting an end to the conversation as he climbed onto the chair between Terese and his father.

"Eggs?" he complained.

"Eggs," Hunter confirmed.

Johnny made a face, but his father was prepared and drowned the scrambled eggs in ketchup before the little boy could say more.

Johnny's hair was, indeed, standing straight up in front the way it had been the night before, but he'd foregone the necktie today in favor of a flannel shirt, jeans and miniature suede work boots.

And as he settled in to eat his breakfast and outline once again for Terese what he had in store for her today, everything suddenly seemed right to her again.

Which, on some level, she knew was a feeling she should probably resist.

Instead she merely sat there and enjoyed it.

Johnny had no problem occupying Terese's day. While Hunter and Willy repaired a tractor engine, the little boy devoted himself to teaching her about the workings of the ranch and demonstrating how to do his own chores.

Terese was astonished by how much the four-year-old knew about the animals and their care, and by what chores he could actually do himself.

He was responsible for feeding the chickens and collecting their eggs, for giving oats to the horses and making sure there was water in their troughs. He had a pony of his own, that he fed, watered, brushed and exercised with great pride. And he did a lot of fetching and carrying for his father and Willy.

Coming from a privileged upbringing in which she'd been shamelessly pampered by nannies and servants, at first she found it somewhat harsh that Johnny wasn't left to four-year-old entertainments. But as the day went on, she saw that he liked helping out, that it gave him a strong sense of himself and his own abilities, and Terese learned that there were merits to it.

Plus, it wasn't as if Johnny didn't have a lot of playtime mixed into the day. He did. There was time for him to show her sword fighting with one of the rails on the paddock fence. Time for him to set up his army men in the barn. Time for him to fashion a number of dirt hills for his toy off-road vehicles to climb and crash.

There was also time for him to introduce Terese to the barn cat and her kittens, time to play with the kittens that liked him better than Terese and crawled all over him, making him roll on the ground in giggles as they did.

There was also time for him to show her the nest of mice he'd found under a shed behind the barn, where he relished lying on his belly watching them—something Terese refused to do, recoiling at the sight when she realized what creatures he'd surprised her with.

Unfortunately there was the sight of something else that she *didn't* recoil from as the day passed. A sight that she couldn't be distracted from even by her interest in everything Johnny did and said. A sight she was drawn to again and again against her will.

And that was the sight of Hunter at work.

Of Hunter leaning over the tractor engine with that taut derriere jutting out into view.

Of Hunter hoisting a bale of hay and making the muscles of those bare forearms bulge.

Of Hunter tossing a pair of leather straps over a broad, straight shoulder.

Of Hunter stretching his back with an arch that jabbed his chiseled chin toward the sky.

Of Hunter combing his fingers through his sun-streaked hair.

Of Hunter walking across the paddock with the long-legged, confident saunter that was almost a swagger.

Even the sight of him wiping grease off his hands engrossed her and caused her to stare almost trance-like until Johnny's voice pulled her out of it.

Okay, so the man was something to behold, she kept telling herself. That didn't mean she had to behold him.

But then, before she knew it, her gaze would snag on something about him, and she'd realize only after several minutes that she was staring again.

By the end of the day, she was very frustrated with herself and her lack of self-control. Frustrated and disgusted.

"You'd think you'd never seen a good-looking man before," she said angrily to her reflection in the bathroom mirror of the cabin when she made a stop there to freshen up before dinner.

But even once she'd brushed out her hair and twisted it into a roll at the back of her head that left a spray of wavy ends at her crown, and reapplied a little mascara and lipgloss, she wasn't convinced that she could practice any more self-control through the evening to come than she had all day long.

The best she could hope for as she went from the cabin to the house in the dusk was that she would eventually get her fill of this man who seemed to attract her attention like metal attracted a magnet and then this phenomena would pass.

And she did hope it would pass. Never in her life had she been so distracted by a man—by any man— and it made her uncomfortable. Not to mention that it just seemed so strange…

When she reached the house Terese did as Hunter had urged her that morning—she walked in without knocking.

"Hi, I'm back," she called as she did, not hesitating to go from the mudroom into the kitchen.

As she expected, Johnny and Hunter were there. Hunter was sitting on one of the chairs at the table pulling on a cowboy boot and Johnny was kneeling on the seat of another chair.

"You want to, don't you, T'rese?" Johnny said, rather than answering her greeting.

He was apparently trying to convince his father of something and enlisting her in the process.

"I don't know if I want to or not since I don't know what we're talking about," she told her nephew.

"I'm not sure how the subject came up," Hunter said before his son had explained, "but I hear you've never roasted marshmallows over a fire."

That only compounded her confusion. "I'm not sure how most of the subjects came up today," she confessed, "but no, I've never roasted marshmallows over a fire."

"So that's why…" Johnny said with precise emphasis on each word as if to make his argument clearer "…we should have a nighttime picnic with a fire so we can do the marshmallows and T'rese can taste 'em."

"Not to mention that then Johnny can have them, too," Hunter said to Terese.

A nighttime picnic. So that was what the little boy was angling for.

Terese didn't have any feelings about it one way or another, though. Because yet again her attention was wandering to Hunter.

He'd showered and shaved since they'd gone their separate ways half an hour earlier, and changed into a pair of darker jeans and a blue Henley shirt. He'd washed his hair, too, because it was slightly damp yet and combed straight back to dry.

It struck Terese that she'd seen him in a variety of clothes, and that it didn't matter how he was dressed, he was appealing in everything. The realization offered her no aid in getting her fill of the sight of him.

"You want to, don't you, T'rese?" Johnny repeated the question he'd greeted her with, saving her from herself as he had on several occasions throughout the day by forcing her to concentrate on him rather than his father.

"That's completely up to your dad," she said, hesitant to support Johnny's side if it was going to cause a problem.

"It'll be fu-un. Like campin'…" Johnny cajoled in a singsong that was obviously designed to be irresistibly tempting. "We can just go to the pond—that's not far—and we can have a fire and make hot dogs and beans and marshmallows."

"You have this all worked out, do you?" Hunter asked.

Johnny just gave him a too-innocent shrug.

Hunter shifted his gold-speckled gaze to Terese. "Well, T'rese," he said, mimicking his son's version of her name. "What do you say? Does that sound like dinner to you?"

"Sure, why not?" Terese conceded, liking it every bit as much when the father said her name that way.

"Then I guess that's what we'll do. Did you bring a warm jacket?" he asked then.

Even though it was late October, the weather had been unseasonably warm and the forecast for the entire week was for more of the same. The evenings cooled down considerably, but Terese hadn't expected to be outside for any length of time after dark so she'd only packed a very light jacket. Which was what she told her host.

"I don't think that'll be enough," he said. "I'll give you something of mine to wear."

"So we're goin'?" Johnny demanded, his excitement on the verge of erupting.

"We're goin'," Hunter confirmed. "But you'll need warmer clothes, too. I want you in your sweatshirt and your field coat."

That was all Johnny needed to hear. He leaped off the chair and ran out of the kitchen, hollering, "I'll be right back!"

"How are you at makin' hot chocolate?" Hunter asked her then with a note of challenge in his voice that was similar to the one last night when he'd let her know he doubted she could cook.

"I think I can handle it," she said.

"You'll have to pour it into a thermos, too."

He was teasing her. The crooked half smile that played around the corner of one side of his mouth gave him away.

"A thermos?" she repeated as if she'd never heard of such a thing.

"It's like a carafe, only with insulation and a screw-on top to keep things inside warm."

"Ah, a carafe. That I understand," she joked. "All I can promise is that I'll picture how our cook would do it and try to master the skill."

Hunter laughed and she liked the sound much too much. "That'll be your job, then. I'll pack up everything else we'll need and get you a coat."

His coat.

Why did the thought of wearing something of Hunter's make her feel as excited as Johnny was by this impromptu picnic?

Terese was beginning to think that breathing manure fumes all day had done something to her sanity.

But all she said was, "I'll get the milk," putting herself into motion before she went any crazier than she already had.

Less than an hour later they were on their way in Hunter's big black pickup.

Hunter was driving and Johnny was safely belted into the center of the bench seat, while Terese sat on the passenger side, snuggled inside the big flannellined jean jacket that Hunter had loaned her. That Hunter had held out for her to slip into.

It still smelled faintly of his aftershave, reminding her that he'd worn it himself. That his broad shoulders and strong back and mighty pectorals and powerful biceps had all been encased in that coat just the way she was at that moment.

But she kept telling herself not to think about it. And especially not to think about the secret little rush it was giving her.

The pond was on Coltrane property and they took a dirt road that began behind the barn and headed out into the open countryside.

Terese was glad Hunter seemed to know where he was going because without any illumination except a full moon and the truck's headlights, she could barely tell where the road actually was. But he didn't seem to have any trouble and within minutes they were pulling up to a small pond beneath a stand of old oak trees that formed a semicircle around the far side of it.

"We can swim here in the summer but not tonight," Johnny informed Terese as they got out of the truck.

Hunter had brought several split logs with them for firewood but he dispatched Johnny to collect some kindling, leaving the truck lights on long enough for that to be accomplished and for the fire to be lit.

Once it was blazing, the truck lights were turned off and they were left to the warm, golden glow of the bonfire. They sat down on logs that acted as benches along the bank of the pond.

"What about cooking hot dogs on the end of a stick over a campfire? Have you ever done that?" Hunter asked Terese as Johnny hunted for just the right sticks for the job and his dad began to unload the picnic basket he'd packed.

"Never," Terese said.

"She go'd to boarding school," Johnny offered from not far away. "But I still don't understand. Don't all schools have boards? In the walls or something?"

It hadn't occurred to Terese that this was how Johnny would take her statement about her schooling.

"Boarding school means that you live at the school," she explained.

"Do you sleep in your desk?" Johnny asked, baffled.

"No, you have school in a school building and you live in a separate building," she said.

"With your family?"

"No, with your classmates. Your family stays at home."

"You don't live home with your mom or dad or anybody?" the little boy said, sounding slightly horrified.

"No."

"And you never got to go campin' or cook on a fire or nothin'?"

Terese smiled. "No, there was no camping or cooking on a fire. We ate all our meals in the dining hall."

"I wouldn't like that," Johnny decided.

"It wasn't a lot of fun," Terese assured him, thinking back on the stuffy, regimented environment where camping or cooking anything over an open fire would have been considered barbaric or unbearably pedestrian.

"What about in the summer?" Johnny persisted when he'd shown her the fine art of poking the sticks through their hot dogs and they were all holding their dinner over the fire. "If you didn't go campin' in the summers, what did you do?"

"I went to Europe most summers. Do you know anything about Europe?"

"Yep," the little boy said authoritatively, surprising her. "My dad's goin' there in how many days now?"

He'd begun that statement answering Terese's question but ended it with a query for his father.

"I don't know that I'm going at all now," Hunter said as if he didn't want to talk about it.

Johnny didn't take note of his father's reply; he simply filled Terese in on the details. "It's a trip to look at some bulls so we can get our herd bigger and tougher. It's 'portant."

"Looks like we're about ready to eat these hot

dogs," Hunter said then, giving Terese the impression that he was trying to change the subject.

But hot dogs and beans were a good distraction for Johnny. He took Terese under his wing and taught her how to pull the hot dog off the stick by using the bun, what condiments were best, and how to eat the beans they'd warmed by placing the opened can just above the flames.

Beans weren't Terese's favorite food but she genuinely enjoyed the hot dog and she let her fellow diners know it.

"I think this was a really good idea," she told them, surprised that Hunter's smile seemed as pleased as his son's.

"Now we get marshmallows!" Johnny announced when they'd finished the main course. "And I can cook everybody's on one stick!"

"Go to it," Hunter allowed.

Johnny stabbed three of the fluffy confections on a single stick, while Terese and Hunter sat back and watched. When the marshmallows were toasty brown, her nephew offered Terese the first one.

Before she could take it, it fell to the ground.

"Oh, no!" Johnny lamented as if it were the end of the world.

Not wanting him to be disappointed, Terese said, "That's okay," picked the marshmallow up, blew it off and popped it into her mouth.

It wasn't the smartest move she'd ever made. There were still grains of soil stuck to it and she couldn't help grimacing slightly when she felt and tasted the residual grit.

Hunter must have caught her expression because she heard him laugh. But Johnny didn't seem to notice.

"Isn't it good?" he asked eagerly.

"It is," Terese assured him after she'd choked it down.

Hunter was sitting on the log that was at a ninety-degree angle to hers and he handed her the bottle of water she'd been drinking, leaning close enough to say, "You could have let that one go and had one of the others."

"I wanted the full experience of what nature has to offer," she lied.

But he knew better and merely laughed again. Not in a way that made fun of her, though. It was more a laugh that said he was enjoying himself. And so was she. In spite of the gritty marshmallow.

Her second taste of Johnny's cooking was an improvement over the first, but after that she'd had enough. Two marshmallows were Hunter's limit as well, but Johnny was a bottomless pit when it came to the sweets. He would have gone on toasting and eating marshmallows until the bag was empty except that his father stopped him at six.

Even so, between the hot chocolate and the marshmallows, the little boy was full of sugar-induced energy that left him unable to sit still once his marshmallow roasting was over, and he turned to jumping off the logs his father and Terese were using as seats.

"How about skipping some rocks in the pond?" Hunter suggested to divert him. "It looks different in the moonlight than it does in the day."

Throwing rocks apparently had an allure all its own because Johnny didn't need more than that to inspire him. He set about collecting rocks until he had all his pockets filled with them. Then he went to the edge of the pond.

"Come and watch, T'rese!" he called to her.

"We can see you from here," Hunter called back before Terese could comply.

She didn't mind that he'd gotten her out of it, though. She liked sitting there by the fire.

With him.

She didn't want to think too much about that.

Besides, he was right; they could see Johnny from where they were.

After watching and complimenting a few of Johnny's tosses, Terese thought she could also take the opportunity to satisfy a bit of curiosity about what her nephew had said earlier in regard to Hunter going to Europe.

"So you have a trip planned?" she asked, glancing from son back to father.

Hunter slid from his log to sit on the ground and lean his back against it instead, bracing his elbows there, too, and stretching his legs out in front of her to avoid the fire.

"I did have," he said. "I was all set to go this coming Saturday, as a matter of fact."

"But now you aren't going?"

"I'm thinkin' no," he said quietly, watching his son and frowning slightly.

"Because of Johnny's health condition?" Terese guessed.

Hunter nodded slowly. "I was going to leave him with Willy and Carla. They think of him as their own and I've never worried about him when he's with them. But now… Well, what if he falls or something—the way he did last week—and starts bleeding and I'm halfway around the world?"

Terese could tell he hadn't been joking when he'd said the discovery of Johnny's hemophilia had shaken him.

"Was Johnny right about the trip being important?" she asked.

"Not as important as Johnny. Nothing is that important."

"No, of course not," she agreed. "But even if the trip isn't as important as Johnny is, if it was important enough to make before, isn't is still important now?"

Hunter raised his eyebrows to concede that. "Sure."

"You were going to improve your stock? Or herd? Or whatever you call it?"

"Either would be right. And yes, that was the idea. There are some new breeds over there that look promising and I wanted to take a look at them, maybe negotiate for a bull. Northwest winters are nothing to sneeze at and anything I can do to make my herd stronger can help get more animals through the snowy months. Plus bigger cows translate to bigger profits at market. The trip and making a buy are things I've been saving for for about two years."

"And you'd cancel the trip when you're just about to make it?"

Hunter merely looked out at his son again, as if that were answer enough.

"What if Johnny were with me?" she said as another thought occurred to her.

The rancher looked back at her, his face gilded by the fire's glow, throwing into greater relief the sharp handsomeness of his features. "What if he were with you?" he repeated.

"I'm just kind of throwing this out there, but, well, I'm already here. What if I stayed and took care of him? Would it make you feel better knowing that his constant companion was his own private blood bank?"

That morsel of levity made Hunter smile. "We're talking about a two-week trip," he said as if he thought that would change her mind.

"Okay."

"Okay?"

"I told you I'm on sabbatical and my time is my own. It isn't as if I *couldn't* stay that long."

Hunter watched his son flinging rocks into the pond again. "I don't know…"

"Why don't you think about it?" Terese urged. "If it would make you feel better, you could still have

Willy and Carla looking after him, too. Then he'd have three baby-sitters instead of two, and one of them could give him a refill if he needed it."

"You wouldn't care if Willy and Carla were still in on it?"

"No, not at all. I'd still get to spend time with Johnny and that's the only thing I'm interested in."

Actually, the more she thought about it, the more she liked the idea of anything that extended her time with her nephew. She'd come to the ranch knowing that she would likely overstay her welcome in a few days and worrying that that would be all she'd ever have with him. Now this seemed to give her an excuse to stay the full week and then have two extra weeks with him on top of it.

"Seriously," she said. "I'd like to do it and you wouldn't have to miss a trip that's been two years in the making. Think it over."

"I just might," he said, as if the longer he mulled the idea the more he really was considering it.

Johnny ran out of rocks then, and both Terese's attention and Hunter's were drawn back to him when he knelt down on the very edge of the pond to run his finger in the water and make motorboat sounds.

"Hey, get out of there," Hunter called to him. Then, to Terese he said, "Maybe we'd better take him home before he goes for a swim."

Terese nodded and Hunter passed along the news to his son.

Johnny grumbled and complained but his father insisted he come away from the pond.

Then Hunter got to his feet and held out his hand to Terese to help her up.

It was clearly something he did out of reflex because the moment he realized what he'd done, he looked as if he'd surprised himself.

Certainly he'd surprised Terese with the sudden possibility of physical contact of any kind.

Before she could respond he pulled his hand back and jammed it into his pocket, muttering, "Oh, you don't need my help," as he turned away from her.

But still Terese couldn't keep from thinking about it as she stood and joined Johnny in gathering things while Hunter put out the fire. She couldn't keep from thinking about the fact that he *had* been inclined to offer that hand. To make that physical contact. As if it might have been something he'd wanted.

She couldn't keep from thinking that if she'd been a little less surprised by it and a little quicker, she could have taken his hand. She could have felt it close around her own. She could have felt the warmth of it. The strength of it. The texture of it.

And she couldn't keep from thinking that that would have been really nice.

In fact, as the three of them piled back in the truck and drove all the way home she couldn't keep from thinking how nice it would have been.

Johnny fell so soundly asleep on that drive back that

he didn't wake up even when the truck stopped. While Hunter carried his son up to put him to bed, Terese stayed lost in her "what-if" musings and carried the picnic basket into the kitchen to empty.

She'd done that when Hunter came downstairs again and by then it was as if the entire thing had never happened.

"You didn't have to do that," he said as she finished cleaning up the remnants of their dinner.

"I don't mind," she assured him. "Did you get Johnny to bed?"

"He never even opened his eyes. The big crash after the sugar rush."

"Combined with a pretty busy day," Terese added, putting rinsed dishes into the dishwasher and steadfastly not looking at Hunter, who was returning condiments to the refrigerator.

"He did plenty of showing off for you, that's for sure."

They both finished at the same time and that left no choice but for her to look at him as he stood behind one of the kitchen chairs, clasping the barrel-back with both big hands.

"It's all right. I don't get all that many men showing off for me," she joked.

"I don't know why not," Hunter countered as their eyes met.

Terese couldn't come up with anything to say to that. Especially not while her eyes clung to his and her thoughts were all on that missed opportunity to have felt her hand in his.

But after a moment it was Hunter who broke the silence.

"You're probably about ready to drop from keeping up with the boy since early this morning."

Terese wondered if that might be her cue to leave, even though it wasn't late.

"I could use a long soak in a bubble bath. And to brush my teeth," she said pointedly.

Hunter laughed. "Well, eating that first marshmallow made Johnny's night, so maybe you can take some comfort in that."

"Some," she agreed.

There was another silence while Terese fostered a tiny hope that Hunter might ask her to stay awhile longer.

But when that didn't happen, she said, "I guess I'll call it a day, then."

"I'll walk you out to the cabin."

"You don't have to," Terese said, even though she was hoping he would, anyway.

Those hopes were met when he let go of the chair and motioned for her to precede him to the mudroom door. "Let a lady walk herself home?" he said as he did. "I can't do that."

Terese led the way out the rear of the house, realizing as she stepped into the night air again that she still had his coat on.

"Oh, I need to give your coat back, too," she commented as they headed for the cabin.

He didn't remark on that fact, though. Instead he said, "I have to take Johnny into the hospital tomorrow at eleven for a follow-up visit. I had to promise him lunch at one of those kiddie places with arcade games and teenagers dressed up in bear costumes to serve bad pizza. Think you can handle it or would you rather beg off?"

"After the grimy marshmallow? I can handle anything," she assured him with a laugh as they reached the cabin and she opened the door.

"The pizza's bad but I guarantee there won't be any dirt on it."

"Okay, then," she said with another laugh.

She stepped inside the cabin, and since she assumed Hunter wouldn't come in, she turned around to face him, finding him leaning against the doorjamb, and, as she had at the end of the previous evening, she once again had the sense that they were ending a date, even though she was well aware that they weren't.

"I enjoyed the night picnic," she said as if they were anyway. "Dirty marshmallow and all."

Hunter's topaz eyes were steady on her and he smiled a lazy smile. "I doubt it compared to what you're used to."

"What I'm used to isn't nearly as much fun," she told him, wondering why her voice had suddenly taken on a quieter, softer tone.

"I'll bet it's a whole lot more sophisticated when a four-year-old hasn't arranged it, though."

"I wouldn't have traded eating marshmallows off the ground for anything."

"You're a good sport," he said in a way that made

it one of the best compliments she'd ever received. Particularly because he said it as if it impressed him.

"Thanks," she said.

For another long moment they just stood there, his eyes holding hers, his expression unreadable.

Then he smiled once more and pushed off the jamb.

"I'll let you get to that bubble bath."

Terese could hardly tell him that she would rather have stayed there with him, just gazing into the topaz brilliance of his eyes, so she merely said, "Your coat," and began to slip it off.

But Hunter was too much of a gentleman to let her do it alone and reached a long arm around her to help. A long arm that brushed her shoulder and set off tiny skitters of something bright and twinkling inside her.

Something bright and twinkling enough that she couldn't resist looking up at him again. At his handsome face. Closer to hers now than it had been before since his arm was still a half circle around her.

Close enough that he could easily have come another few inches and pressed his mouth to hers.

Especially when her chin tipped upward on its own.

And his tipped downward...

But it was only for a split second before he pulled the coat the rest of the way off and straightened up, as if his own actions had surprised him.

"Breakfast'll be at eight again," he informed her slightly tersely, then he turned to go back to the house as if nothing at all had passed between them.

And maybe nothing *had* passed between them, Terese thought as she watched him go. Maybe she'd just imagined that brief moment and kissing hadn't been on his mind the way it had been on hers.

But she didn't think she'd only imagined it.

She *hoped* she hadn't only imagined it.

It just felt so good to think she hadn't.

Four

"Now this is what I like to see!"

Terese was walking down a corridor of Portland General Hospital the next day with Hunter and Johnny when an older woman and a man about Hunter's age turned a corner in front of them. The moment the older woman caught sight of Johnny and his father, recognition dawned and her face lit up with a smile.

"This is definitely what I like to see—Mr. John Coltrane, looking healthy and happy and none-the-worse-for-wear after his adventure last week," she clarified. Then, after rubbing the top of Johnny's head, she raised her gaze and said, "Hello, Hunter."

"Leslie," Hunter said warmly in return. And to the

man who was with her, he said, "Morgan, good to see you."

"Hi," the man responded simply enough.

Johnny spotted a fish tank in a waiting area beside them and, apparently assuming the grown-ups were going to chat, he ran off to take a closer look at the fish. His dad said, "Terese, I'd like you to meet Leslie Logan. She's one of Children's Connection's most valuable assets. And Morgan Davis, the agency's director. Leslie, Morgan, this is Terese Warwick."

"You're the woman who came to Johnny's rescue last week," Leslie Logan said before Hunter had a chance. Then, to explain how she knew that, she added, "The hospital is like a small town. A good story travels fast. Especially when it involves one of our own. And since Hunter adopted Johnny through Children's Connection that just automatically makes him and Johnny a part of us."

"Not to mention," Morgan put in, "that Hunter has stayed active in the foundation and with PAN."

Terese didn't know what the foundation or PAN were but she didn't have a chance to do more than smile and say, "Nice to meet you both," before the older woman spoke to Hunter again, this time with a more serious edge to her voice.

"You were so lucky that Johnny averted tragedy last week and is doing well."

"Don't I know it," Hunter agreed.

"Something happening to your child takes a horrible toll. You know my firstborn, Robbie, was abducted when he was only a little boy and we've never seen him again. It changed my husband and me. It changed our marriage. It changed everything. Forever. The loss of a child isn't something you ever get over. I'm just glad you didn't have to learn that firsthand."

The loss of her child was clearly a pain the older woman still carried with her after what had to have been many years, and Terese felt very sorry for her.

"I count my blessings every day," Hunter assured Leslie Logan.

"But on a happier note," she said more cheerily, "it seems Morgan and his wife Emma are going to join the ranks of parenthood. They've applied with the agency to adopt a baby of their own."

"Congratulations," Terese said to Morgan.

"Good for you," Hunter contributed enthusiastically. "Any idea how long it'll take?"

"There'll be some time involved yet. We've just started the procedure. Maybe by the start of summer next year, if we're as lucky as you've been."

"I'll keep my fingers crossed for you," Hunter promised.

"We'd probably better let you get going," Leslie Logan said then. "You wouldn't be here with that beautiful boy of yours if you didn't have a reason and we're keeping you."

"We're on our way for an appointment with his doctor. Just a follow-up," Hunter confirmed.

"Will we see you at the PAN meeting tomorrow night?" Leslie asked.

"I'll be there."

"Good." The older woman glanced at Johnny, who was tapping on the fish-tank glass. "Nice to see you again, Master Johnny."

"You, too," the little boy answered perfunctorily, without taking his eyes off the fish.

The adults said goodbye and then Hunter informed his son that they had to get going. The little boy reluctantly rejoined his father and Terese.

"What's PAN?" Terese asked as they continued on their way.

"PAN stands for Parents Adoption Network. It's an organization that's part of the agency. I've belonged since I adopted Johnny."

"And the foundation?"

"It's connected with the hospital. Leslie Logan and her husband are major benefactors, not to mention that Leslie does a considerable amount of volunteer work. The foundation is an umbrella that encompasses a fertility treatment center, counseling for childless couples, support groups, financial support for orphanages around the world and, of course, the adoption agency."

"I see," Terese said as they came to the door of the office they needed.

But before they went in, Hunter's focus switched to his son. "Remember," he warned. "Lunch at Pokey's Pizza is only if you behave in here."

"No shots, right?" Johnny said as if to make sure his father kept up his part of the deal, too.

"I don't think there will be any shots, no."

"Okay," the little boy said. Then, in an aside to his father, he added, "And T'rese can't see me in my underwear."

Terese fought a laugh but Hunter wasn't as tactful. He didn't bother to conceal his amusement. "Deal. I won't let Terese see you in your underwear."

Then, to Terese as he opened the door, Hunter winked and said, "We wouldn't want to ruin his suave, sophisticated image, after all."

Johnny's doctor's visit went well even though the little boy had to have blood drawn. He sat on his father's lap, held the hand Terese offered him, and beyond wide eyes and a quivering lip, he bravely managed not to cry.

For that he was rewarded not only with the promised trip to Pokey's Pizza, but Hunter allowed him the entire afternoon there.

Of course, after they'd eaten lunch and the three of them began playing the arcade games, she could tell Hunter was enjoying himself as much as his son was.

She was interested to see the interaction of father and son at play, though. She'd seen it at work the day before—the way Hunter had been willing to spare the time to teach Johnny small tasks, Hunter's patience when the child hadn't done something exactly right, letting Johnny know that he trusted him enough to give him responsibilities of his own. Now she was curious to see how the two related to each other away from the ranch work.

Hunter didn't disappoint her. His parenting techniques when it came to recreation were every bit as good. He managed to stimulate just the right amount of competitive spirit in Johnny while maintaining all the fun—just enough to make Johnny want to try hard to give his father a good game when it came to tossing the basketball or the softball. There was no question that Hunter was holding back but he didn't let it show to his son, and the result was that Johnny's self-esteem grew right before her eyes when the little boy ended up winning.

Terese played a few games with her nephew but she wasn't good at them and actually preferred watching.

Watching Johnny.

Or at least she told herself that she preferred watching Johnny. In truth, she did a whole lot of watching Hunter, too. And she definitely preferred that to tossing rings over pegs or trying to hit monster heads that popped up through holes in a table.

But then how could she not, when he had on a beige Western shirt that glided over the muscles of his honed upper body, and a pair of khaki-colored jeans slung low on his hips and cupping his derriere just enough to accentuate how terrific it was every time he leaned over?

And no matter how often she told herself it was Hunter's parenting skills she was admiring, deep down she knew those parenting skills—no matter how good they were—weren't the only things she appreciated as the afternoon passed.

* * *

It was nearly six by the time they returned to the ranch. Terese let Hunter and Johnny go into the house alone so she could have a few minutes in the cabin to freshen up before dinner.

She'd worn jeans and a pale blue sweater set and she didn't change clothes, but she did refresh her mascara and blush, and take her hair out of the rubber band that held it at her nape. Once she'd brushed it, she twisted it into a figure-eight knot at the back of her head.

Then, judging herself unlikely to stop traffic but sufficiently presentable, she left the cabin, wondering at the fact that she'd just spent the entire day with her nephew and Hunter and still couldn't wait to get back to them.

But it wasn't only Johnny and Hunter who were in the kitchen when she went in through the mudroom door. Willy and Carla were there, too.

"Carla brought us a ham, cheese and potato casserole," Hunter informed Terese when the greetings were finished. "I'm twisting their arms to make them stay and eat with us."

"Good," Terese said, for the most part meaning it. She genuinely liked the ranchhand and his wife, it was just that there was also a tiny drop of disappointment that now she would have to share Johnny and Hunter. She knew that was uncalled for.

The table was already set for three—Terese assumed Carla had done that, too—so Terese set two more places while Carla took the casserole from the oven. The other woman also took an already prepared salad out of the refrigerator, and everyone sat down to eat.

Small talk occupied the meal. Terese learned that Carla frequently brought Hunter and Johnny dinner that she left for them when she picked up Willy after a day of work. And that Carla and Willy didn't usually stay despite the fact that Johnny liked it when they did.

Carla and Willy were also anxious to know what the doctor had said about Johnny and were relieved to hear that he was fine, that his blood count was good, and that, with the exception of being cautious, he could go on about his everyday business just the way he always had.

With four people for cleanup after they'd all eaten, the kitchen was shipshape in no time and then Carla and Willy insisted—in the face of Johnny's best efforts to get them to linger—that they had to go home.

"He's just trying to get out of taking a bath," Hunter said as Johnny huffed off in a pout to engross himself in his toys in the living room and Hunter and Terese walked Carla and Willy to the front door.

But rather than saying a simple good-night once they were there, Hunter turned to Terese and said, "After a day to think about it, is your offer still good to stay with Johnny if I go through with my trip to Europe?"

He hadn't mentioned a word about that all day and

Terese certainly hadn't expected him to bring it up now. But since he had and she hadn't changed her mind, she didn't hesitate to say, "Absolutely."

"Well," Hunter said, "I talked it over with Carla and Willy before you came in tonight and they think I should go, too."

"You can't *not* go," Carla said emphatically. Then, to Terese, the other woman added, "He did this after Margee died, too. He was overly cautious and didn't want to let Johnny out of his sight for fear something else bad would happen. But I told him that between the three of us we'll watch Johnny like a hawk."

"We will," Terese assured Hunter.

"And even if something does come up," Willy contributed, aiming his comment at Hunter, "you can get on a plane and be home in no time. But not to go at all? You have too much riding on this to just blow it off."

Hunter didn't disagree with that. But he did look into the living room at his son for a moment before he finally seemed to make his decision.

"I guess I am being a little paranoid," he said.

"Yes, you are," Carla confirmed. "Now say you'll go. You'll probably worry yourself to death, but say you'll go, anyway."

Hunter laughed at his friend's bossiness. "Okay, okay. If Terese really will stay so she's nearby if he needs blood, I'll go."

"And everything will be fine. You'll see," Carla decreed.

The matter seemed to be solved then, and, with that accomplished, the couple said good-night and left.

There were things Terese wanted to say to Hunter once they were gone but before she had the chance, he began the tug-of-war with Johnny to get him to bed.

It wasn't until an hour later, after the efforts of both Terese and Hunter had the little boy down for the night and Terese was helping Hunter pick up Johnny's toys in the living room that she finally found the opportunity.

"You know," she said then, "it's perfectly normal to feel the way you do about Johnny right now. And the way you felt after your wife died. Some things are like emotional earthquakes. Remember when you said the other night that last week's ordeal with Johnny shook you? That's exactly what happens. The foundation of things feels shaky for a while, until you get used to whatever changes come out of those emotional earthquakes and things settle down again. Right now it's as if you're on edge, waiting for aftershocks."

"Is this the psychology professor talking?" he asked with a hint of amusement to his voice.

Terese smiled at him from across the coffee table where they were putting puzzle pieces back in a box. "It is," she confirmed.

"Was it the psychology professor talking before, too, when you were tiptoeing around that stuff about adoptive parents being insecure if the birth family is in the picture?"

"Then, too. But both things are true, you know."

"I'm sure they are," he allowed. But he still didn't seem to want to discuss either of them.

In Terese's experience that wasn't an unusual response. When people found out what field her education and training were in, they either wanted a quick therapy session or they went to extremes to avoid it so she didn't analyze them. Obviously Hunter was in the second category. But that was fine with her. The last thing she wanted to be was his therapist.

Then Hunter veered even farther away from that by turning the conversation toward her job. "So you teach psychology, huh? How did that come about?"

There was amusement in Terese's tone this time. "I'll bet you're figuring there are years and years of psychoanalysis in my background that sucked me in."

"Is that the way it was?"

"Nope," she said, mimicking his periodic answer to things she asked him. "I just developed an interest in it when I took my first psychology class in my freshman year of college. Actually, I realized I had spent my life sort of standing on the sidelines, observing people and their behavior, thinking about what made them tick, and when I discovered a class that talked about that, I also discovered my niche."

They'd finished putting away Johnny's puzzle and the rest of his toys, and Hunter sat on one end of the sofa, angled toward the center, his arm stretched across the top of the back cushion.

There was no hint that he was ready for her to go out to the cabin tonight. In fact, something about his attitude seemed to say he expected her to sit, too. So that was what Terese did—sit on the couch but at the opposite end.

It must have been what he'd had in mind because he merely went on with their conversation. "Don't take this wrong, but I'm kind of surprised that you work at all."

She knew what he was thinking—that she was a trust-fund baby who didn't need to earn a living. "I don't do it for the money. I do it because I enjoy it."

"Does your sister work?"

"Eve? Unless you count working at being Eve and keeping up with the latest fashions and hairstyles and makeup, no. But maybe if I looked the way she does instead of the way I do—"

He cut her off before she could finish that. "That day at your house your sister made a not-too-nice comment about the way you look. You don't buy into that, do you?"

"Into the fact that I'm not as attractive as Eve? That I'm the lesser twin? It isn't a matter of buying into it. It's a fact of life."

His brow creased into a frown. "You look different than she does, but the 'lesser-twin'? You have to be kidding."

He sounded as if he genuinely couldn't fathom that.

"Eve is beautiful," she said.

"Beauty is in the eye of the beholder," he countered. "Or maybe 'beauty is only skin-deep' would be a better platitude. Either way, I don't see your sister as beautiful. But you…"

He was studying her openly and it made Terese uncomfortable. Especially since she was sure he was going to find all kinds of flaws.

But then he said, "You have beautiful hair and skin like fresh cream. Your eyes glisten like moonlight on a still lake. You remind me of a spring morning when everything is clear and bright and new…." He shook his head, still keeping his eyes on her. "I like the way you look. I like it a whole lot better than the way your sister looks."

There was something in his voice that made her believe this was actually how he felt, although it didn't convince her that she was more attractive than her sister. She thought that Hunter's opinions were just colored negatively by Eve's actions and positively by her own. And yet, his opinion of her still made her happier than he would ever know.

And more embarrassed. She could feel her cheeks heating, and she knew they had to be beet red.

But if Hunter noticed, he didn't comment on it. He just continued.

"Plus, unless I've missed something, you have a whole lot more going for you than your sister in every other regard," he said.

"I'm just a teacher," she demurred.

"A college professor, which is the top-of-the-heap teacher."

Terese merely shrugged, unsure what to say to that.

"So why did you decide to teach, anyway? Why not do therapy or counseling?"

Terese had no idea when he'd gone from talking about her appearance to talking about her job but she was grateful for the change of topic nonetheless.

"The academics just appealed to me," she told him. "I teach and do research—"

"What kind of research?"

"I know when I say that, people picture test tubes. But a psychologist's research is interviewing people. For instance, before I went on sabbatical I did follow-up research on teenagers who had been taking psychotropic drugs for ten years, beginning before the age of eight. That meant locating kids for the study and talking to them about where they are now, physically and mentally, and trying to determine whether being on medication has been beneficial enough to warrant the side effects. It's that kind of research."

"And why are you on sabbatical now?"

He sounded genuinely interested and his focus on her was still so intent that Terese didn't think he was merely being polite.

"I'm finishing my doctoral dissertation," she said.

Hunter's eyebrows arched. "You'll be Dr. Warwick?"

"It'll be a Ph.D., but yes, I'll be Dr. Warwick. On the school roster and to my students at least, though I don't think it will matter to anyone else."

"Dr. Warwick," Hunter repeated. "And you think you're the lesser twin? That's a whole lot more than your sister can say. I know I'm impressed," he said, but with a hint of teasing that made it clear he wasn't intimidated by her accomplishments the way some men she'd encountered had been. She liked that.

"What about you?" she asked then. "I know the ranch has been in your family for generations but how did you and Willy come to work it instead of you and that brother you mentioned before?"

One of his eyebrows hiked toward his hairline and he pointed a long, thick index finger at her. "You were paying attention," he said as if it flattered him that she'd been listening close enough to what he'd said to remember it.

"I confess, I really was paying attention, yes. You said that Willy is closer to you than your brother—from which I took it that you have at least one brother."

Hunter didn't comment on his familial relationships, though. It was the question about how he'd come to be a rancher that he addressed.

"I started working alongside my father and grandfather like Johnny is now at about the same age. And I loved it just the way he does. Being outside in the fresh air, it was more like play than work. Then, as I got older I started to appreciate moving through my day at my own pace, not having a boss breathing down my neck. I didn't mind getting my hands dirty or having to start before dawn or working weekends and holidays—you know, animals have to be fed, cows have to be milked no matter what. It all just fit," he concluded.

"So you found your niche at four years old and never wavered?" Terese said with some awe.

"I wavered. Or maybe it was teenage rebellion. But

yeah, there was a period when I tried out a different lifestyle and considered doing things other than ranching."

"For instance?" Terese said to urge him into details.

"I went to college at the University of Colorado in Boulder. That's hardly a rural setting. During those four years I worked to pay my tuition by being a night watchman in a big office building. All cooped up five nights a week from six in the evening until three in the morning."

"I'm guessing the 'cooped-up' part is what got to you?"

"Mmm. It was good for studying, but I definitely got tired of being stuck inside. Only not before I thought about being a lawyer or a businessman."

Terese smiled at that. There he was, dressed in his jeans, Western shirt and cowboy boots, with muscles nudging the confines of his clothes and his rugged handsomeness kissed by the sun, looking every inch the cowboy, and she just couldn't picture him as anything else. Certainly not as an attorney or an executive.

"What?" he challenged as if he could read her thoughts. "You don't think I could be a lawyer or a corporate muckety-muck?"

"I'm just surprised that either of those occupations ever appealed to you," she said to cover her tracks.

"I was under the influence."

"Of what?"

"The other two guys who worked my shift. They were both two years ahead of me, so while I finished my bachelor's degree, one of them went on to an MBA program, while the other went to law school."

"And they nearly convinced you to follow in their footsteps?"

"I don't know how *nearly* it was, but I admit that they had me thinkin'. The law student was sure he'd end up on the Supreme Court, and the business major was determined to wow Wall Street. That made coming back here to work the ranch pale by comparison."

"And you were an impressionable eighteen- to twenty-two-year-old."

"I was," he said with an irresistible half grin.

"So what happened to pull you back to the ranch?" Terese asked, trying not to go limp at the sight of that sexy, charming smile he flashed at her.

"A couple of things. Family things, partly. My grandfather died. That wasn't unexpected since his health had been failing pretty consistently for the last year or more of his life. But when he died that left my dad with only my brother to help around here and then there was some stuff with my brother…"

Apparently the *stuff* with his brother wasn't good because Hunter's brow furrowed at just the mention of it.

But he didn't seem inclined to explain because after a moment's pause, he went past it. "Anyway, about the time I was ready to graduate, my dad really needed me back here and to tell you the truth I'd sort of mentally tried on the lawyer bit and the businessman bit, and I knew they weren't right for me. I was itching to get outside again."

"And you've been here ever since?"

"Ever since."

"Without any regrets or secret wishes that maybe you *had* become a lawyer or a businessman?"

That made him chuckle. "Absolutely no secret wishes or regrets. Once I got my hands dirty again, I knew there was nothin' else for me. It's like getting away for a while, even considering doing something else, made me appreciate this all the more. Just remembering that I ever thought about those other things seems crazy now. Ranchin' really is my niche, as you put it. I love everything about it."

"Which is why you want to improve your herd and keep things going," Terese concluded. "And why it's good that you decided to go on your trip."

He nodded, but he did it so slowly she could tell he still had reservations.

Whether it was those reservations or the fact that they'd been talking a long while and the hour had gotten late, they seemed to have reached a lull. A lull that Terese thought she should act on before she overstayed her welcome.

So she stood and said, "I'll bet missing most of today's work means you have that much more to do tomorrow so I should let you get some rest."

Hunter didn't refute that. In fact, he confirmed it by standing, too.

"Speaking of tomorrow," he said as Terese led the way to the kitchen, "Willy and I have some fences to fix at the far end of the place. Mendin' fences is Johnny's least favorite of my jobs. He gets bored out on the range without much to do. So I was wondering if you might want to stay around here with him? He's been pestering me to let him draw faces on a bunch of the pumpkins he'll get me to carve for him, and he has a Halloween video I haven't had time to let him watch. You could keep him occupied doing some of that, if you wouldn't mind...."

"Mending fences does sound a little on the boring side," Terese acknowledged. "But I'd love to do pumpkins and watch the Halloween video. Halloween wasn't a holiday we did much with in boarding school. The headmaster said it was a low-class, heathen holiday. This will give me a chance to experience it."

"No camping and no Halloween? What kind of a childhood did you have, anyway?"

Terese laughed. "A very stuffy one," she admitted.

They'd gone through the kitchen to the mudroom by then and Hunter reached around in front of her to open the door. But once she'd gone through it, he followed her outside. Apparently walking her to the cabin was becoming enough of a habit for him to do it without announcing that he was going to the way he had on the previous nights.

But Terese certainly wasn't going to complain. She appreciated the gentlemanly courtesy. As well as the few more minutes it gave her with him.

"I hope you didn't feel pressured into making that doctor's appointment today," Hunter said as they strolled through the balmy October air in the quiet of the yard.

During Johnny's visit, the hematologist had aggressively suggested that since hemophilia was passed from mother to son, Terese should be tested to determine if, like her twin, she carried the gene.

Terese hadn't been enthusiastic about it, even though it only required a blood test, but Johnny's doctor had been so insistent that she'd finally conceded and made an appointment for herself for early the following week.

"He was probably right," she told Hunter in answer to his concern that she'd felt pressured. "It's information I should have, even if it doesn't ever become relevant."

They'd reached the cabin and she opened the door and turned on the overhead light, stepping just inside and turning to find him leaning one broad shoulder against the jamb the same way he had the night before, his hands hidden in the pockets of his low-slung jeans.

"Why wouldn't it become relevant?" he asked. "Don't you want kids of your own?"

"I'd love to have kids of my own. But I doubt I'll ever have the chance."

Hunter frowned in confusion. "Why not?"

That wasn't a subject she wanted to get into right then so she merely shrugged. "It's complicated. But I just don't think marriage and family are in the cards for me."

"This isn't more of that 'lesser twin' thing, is it?"

Terese repeated the shrug. "And some prior experience," she said more to herself than to him.

Hunter was studying her again and he shook his head. "I don't know where this is all coming from but you're so damn wrong..."

His eyes were delving deeply into hers and for no reason Terese understood she felt mesmerized by their gold-streaked intensity. So mesmerized that words escaped her and the only thing she could think about was the same thing she'd thought about at the end of the last two evenings—what it might be like to have him kiss her.

But theirs wasn't that kind of relationship, she told herself.

Still, she was looking up into that ruggedly beautiful male face, into those topaz-colored eyes that seemed to be bathing her in a warm glow, and she couldn't escape the sense that him kissing her was what should be happening at that moment.

And then, suddenly, it was.

Suddenly he was leaning forward. She was tilting her chin up. And their mouths just somehow met as her eyes drifted shut.

He was kissing her.

His lips were over hers, parted just slightly, sweet and sexy at the same time.

And she was kissing him back.

She was letting her own lips relax and open just slightly. She was letting her head move just a little in answer to his movements.

Even as her mind spun with the pure amazement that this was happening, her senses were registering the feel of that kiss, the smell of his aftershave, the heat of his breath against her skin....

Oh, what a kiss it was!

A great kiss. A kiss that she willed to last and last.

To last long enough for him to put his arms around her. Long enough for him to pull her against him. Long enough for him to press his hands to her back and give her the excuse to press hers to the muscles of his. To have her breasts against the hard wall of his chest and the rest of her body running the length of his...

But the kiss didn't last long enough for any of that.

Instead, Hunter eased into ending it, slowly straightening up again and returning to just peering down into her eyes.

"I'm sorry," he said then. "I shouldn't have done that."

"Yes, you should have," she blurted out before she realized she was going to say anything at all.

She could feel her face suffuse with color again, but the comment and the blush only made Hunter smile.

"I should have?" he asked.

"I just meant it was okay," she said, making a desperate effort to regroup.

His smile grew even bigger. "Only *okay?*" he teased as if she'd given him a rating.

"Well, maybe a *little* better than okay," she allowed, finally getting hold of herself enough to play along.

Hunter chuckled, maintaining his search of her eyes for a moment longer as a number of emotions seemed to war in his expression, leaving Terese thinking that he'd surprised himself as much as he'd surprised her with that kiss.

Then, as if those warring emotions had settled or resigned themselves, he said, "Tomorrow night I have the PAN meeting."

"I remember."

"It's at seven and shouldn't take longer than an hour or so. Willy and Carla are baby-sitting Johnny—"

"And you want me to, instead?"

That made him smile slightly. "No, they've promised him an evening of making caramel apples and anybody who gets in the way of that is in for trouble. Actually, I was going to ask you if you'd like to go with me to the meeting—not that you'd be interested in it, but you could read a magazine or something while it goes on—and then, when it's over, maybe we could have dinner? The meeting is in one of the conference rooms at the hospital and there's a pretty good seafood restaurant nearby. Do you eat seafood?"

"I do," she confirmed as her mind spun wildly in response to this turn of events.

"After last night's dinner of hot dogs and marshmallows dropped in the dirt, and pizza with pineapple on it for lunch today, I think I owe you a nice meal," he went on to say.

"You don't. You don't owe me anything."

"I'd just like to make it up to you, then."

Or was he simply occupying her time since both he and Johnny already had plans?

"Don't feel as if you have to entertain me if there are other things going on for you and Johnny. I—"

"I was just thinking that it might be nice to have dinner. Together. *I'd* like to, anyway."

"So would I," Terese was quick to assure him when it became evident he thought she was dragging her feet. Then, with more control of herself, she said, "It sounds good. The fish and having dinner together."

He smiled at her once more, again studying her face, probing her eyes for a moment before he broke it off and stepped back out of the doorway. "Then we're on," he confirmed.

"Okay."

"See you in the morning," he said, taking one hand out of his pocket to wave as he turned to go.

"See you in the morning," Terese answered, forcing herself to retreat far enough inside the cabin to close the door rather than standing there watching him the way she was inclined to do.

But even when Hunter was out of her sight he still wasn't out of her mind.

And neither was that kiss he'd just given her.

Or the fact that he'd asked her to dinner the next night.

And while the last few minutes of that evening had left her confused, they'd also left her smiling so big it almost hurt.

Five

"Hey, good news about Johnny yesterday, huh?"

It was one of the first things Willy said to Hunter on Wednesday morning. They'd loaded Hunter's truck and were headed for the fences that needed repair.

"It'd be better news if they said he didn't have hemophilia at all, but given that that's not going to happen, yeah, it was good news that he came through last week's scare without any more problems," Hunter allowed.

"At least now you know what's goin' on with him and where to get blood in an emergency," Hunter's longtime friend said.

"True. And Terese would never turn him down."

"No, she seems pretty fond of him. Pretty fond of you, too, maybe…"

Willy had added that last part under his breath, but Hunter heard it, anyway. He took his eyes off the deserted country road he was driving and glanced at his passenger. "What?" he said as if the suggestion were ridiculous.

"Carla thinks she can feel vibes when the two of you are together—you and Terese. Whatever *vibes* means."

Hunter didn't tell his friend that he had some understanding of what Carla meant. Or that Carla might be right. Or that the fact that there might be vibes between himself and Terese had thrown him all off-kilter. He just said, "What'd Carla say?"

"Only the vibes thing." It was Willy's turn to look over at Hunter. "Is she right?"

Hunter didn't answer. He only shrugged.

"So there *is* something goin' on?" Willy asked, sounding surprised.

"There's not really anything going on…" Hunter hedged, thinking about the kiss he and Terese had shared the night before. The kiss that had almost happened the night before that. The kiss that he'd been itching for and still should probably not have let happen at all.

"You like her," Willy said as if he were seeing it for the first time.

"Sure, well enough," Hunter said noncommittally. "Terese is a nice person. A world different than her sister."

"Her sister who is also Johnny's birth mother."

Was there a criticism in Willy pointing that out? Or

was it just that that fact bothered Hunter so much that he was overly sensitive to it?

Hunter couldn't be sure. So he didn't take issue with it; he only confirmed it. "Right, Terese is a world different than her sister, who is also Johnny's birth mother."

"But they're still sisters," Willy persisted.

"Yeah."

"And you've got a little thing for the nice sister?" Willy asked.

"I don't know," Hunter answered, opting to be honest when he could easily have denied it and put his friend off the track. "But I know that it isn't what you'd call the most ideal situation."

"That's putting it mildly," Willy observed.

Silence reigned for a moment before Willy spoke again, this time treading somewhat more carefully. "This is the first time this has happened since Margee. You maybe being attracted to a woman."

"Yeah," Hunter agreed equally as tentatively.

Regardless of how tentative it was, it still seemed to solidify the possibility for his friend. "So it *is* happening?" Willy asked.

"I don't know. Maybe something is."

"Something like what?"

"I don't know," Hunter repeated once more. "I just…I don't know. I guess I'm sort of enjoying having her around."

"Her in particular or just having a woman around the house again?"

Hunter hadn't considered that, and he did now, hoping that maybe his friend had hit on an easier answer to whatever it was that was happening with him when Terese was around. Hoping that it wasn't Terese herself, that it was just having a woman around again that was appealing to him.

But no matter how he looked at it, he came to the same conclusion. "It's Terese in particular," he confessed.

"Oh," Willy said. "How so?"

Hunter thought about that, too, wanting to figure it all out. Wanting to know what the hell was happening to him.

Then, despite realizing that he was beginning to sound like a broken record, he once more began with, "I don't know. She's just not what I expected. Even after she came with me to the hospital last week, and I could tell she was nicer than her sister, I still thought she'd be… Well, stuck-up or stiff or so snobby and straitlaced that she'd get on my nerves."

"But she isn't stuck-up or stiff or snobby or straitlaced," Willy said, as if he'd realized that, too.

"No, she isn't any of that. There's no doubt that she didn't grow up the way we did, that she's from a whole different world, but she's still down-to-earth and open to things she hasn't done or experienced before. She doesn't turn her nose up at anything. Or look down it at anyone, either. She's interested in things other than herself. She's open to learning what she doesn't know. She listens—to me and to Johnny even when he's talking her ear off. She's honest—she'll answer any question either of us asks her. She's pleasant and funny and Johnny and I both have a great time with her and—"

Hunter knew he was going on and on, and he cut himself off, shrugging and saying yet again, "I don't know, it's just been...I've just liked having her around."

And he was missing having her with them right at that moment, but he didn't tell his friend that. In fact, he could hardly believe it himself.

"So you've got a little thing for her," Willy concluded. "And Carla thinks Terese has a little thing for you."

Hunter cast his ranch hand a glance out of the corner of his eye. "I thought you said Carla didn't say anything except the vibe thing?"

"That was part of the vibe thing. That Terese steals a lot of looks at you when you don't notice it, and brightens up when you come into the room, and gets real interested whenever you're talking or anyone else is talking about you. Stuff that made Carla think Terese has a little thing for you."

A *little thing* that had caused her to kiss him back the night before...

But Hunter didn't say that. He just rolled his eyes and shook his head. "Terese is a nice person, maybe Carla is taking that for more than it really is."

"What if Carla isn't taking it for more than it really is? What if Terese does have a little thing for you and you have a little thing for her? Would you let it go anywhere?"

He'd already let it go to kissing. That was letting it

go somewhere. And as much as he'd liked it, as much as he'd wanted it to last longer than he'd allowed it to, as much as he hadn't been able to think about too many other things since it had happened, he still knew he probably shouldn't have done it at all.

"Letting it go anywhere would be complicated," he said, which, along with thinking about that kiss and how much he wanted to kiss her again, had also been on his mind nonstop. "Complicated and probably not the best idea," he added.

He felt Willy turn to stare at him. "Complicated and not the best idea?" the ranch hand parroted. "Every time Carla's tried to fix you up with someone you've gone into a huge song and dance about the decision you made when Margee died and how your love life is totally and completely on hold. But now, with Terese, it's just complicated and not the best idea?"

"Well, it is complicated and not the best idea."

"Sure. But what I'm gettin' at is, why aren't you just saying a flat no, the way you have with other women?"

Because this woman was different. And not just different than he'd expected or different than her nasty sister. But different in what she was stirring in him. Things that hadn't been stirred in him since Margee's death.

But once again Hunter merely said, "I don't know."

"Yeah, you have a little thing for her, all right," Willy concluded for himself.

"Not saying I do, but what if I did?"

"Definitely complicated," the ranch hand decreed.

"With you and Carla?" Hunter asked, testing the waters.

"Not with me," Willy said. "I want to see you happy, period. With Carla? She likes Terese and I think she'd be okay with it. It's just tough for her to see you with someone other than her best friend. But complicated because of who Terese is."

Complicated and not the best idea, Hunter repeated to himself.

In spite of how complicated it was, in spite of anything personal happening between the two of them not being a good idea—maybe even being about the worst idea there ever was—it didn't change anything for him.

He was still thinking about her, no matter how hard he tried not to. He was still itching to be with her whenever he wasn't. He was still remembering how much he'd enjoyed sitting and talking to her the previous evening. He was still recalling how much he'd wanted to kiss her the night before last and last night.

He was still thinking about that kiss and how much he'd enjoyed it.

And he was still thinking about how much he wanted to do it again.

Not even the complications, not even the solemn swearing-off of a love life that he'd done after his wife's death managed to stop any of it.

Terese's day with Johnny flew by. They drew faces on six pumpkins and Terese let herself be talked into carving two of them—something she was inexperienced and very bad at, but her nephew didn't seem to notice.

They also used Johnny's crayons, watercolor paints and markers to make Halloween decorations that they hung up in the living room and the kitchen, in Johnny's room, and in the cabin so Terese wouldn't be left out. Then they sat together on the sofa with a bag of microwave popcorn and watched animated Halloween movies.

Through it all Terese tried to concentrate solely on her nephew. There was no doubt that she was as enamored of him, as fascinated and entertained by him, as she could possibly be. In spite of that, it still wasn't easy to keep her thoughts from wandering to Hunter. To the way Hunter looked, the way he sounded, the things he'd said and how he'd said them. To Hunter and the kiss that had ended the previous evening. To Hunter and the dinner they were having tonight…

And then Hunter and Willy returned from mending fences, and Terese turned Johnny over to his father so she could go to the cabin to get ready for her night out. And even the marginal success she'd had warding off those thoughts of Hunter was lost. Because without any distraction at all, it was impossible to keep the man out of her head.

Instead, as she stepped under the spray of a steamy shower, those thoughts of Hunter kept her constant company. Only now, for no reason she understood, insecurities she was all too familiar with began to pummel her with questions.

Questions about *why* Hunter had kissed her.

About *why* he'd asked her to have dinner with him.

She didn't want to be jaded, but experience had taught her some harsh lessons. Lessons about attractive men who seemed to show an interest in her. Lessons about not being too easily convinced that they really were interested in *her*...

So why *had* Hunter kissed her last night and invited her to dinner tonight? she asked herself as she coated her hair with conditioner and then began to use a honey-and-vanilla-scented body scrub on the rest of her.

She wanted to believe that both the kiss and the impending dinner had simply come out of an attraction to her. She wanted to believe that he enjoyed her company, that he liked her.

But she also kept remembering another time when she'd believed those things of another man. A man who wasn't even as strikingly good-looking as Hunter. A man who hadn't exuded as much of the pure, innate sensuality that Hunter did. But a man who, like Hunter, could have had any woman he wanted.

And she'd been wrong.

So maybe, a little voice in the back of her mind said, she shouldn't be so quick to believe that that kiss had come from Hunter being attracted to her, or that tonight's invitation to dinner had come from him merely wanting to spend some time alone with her.

But if he had kissed her and suggested dinner tonight for some other reason, then what was that other reason? she wondered as she let the shower's spray rinse her body and hair, then wrapped a towel around her head and used another to dry off.

The only reason she could come up with was what she considered the worst-case scenario.

Hunter owned a ranch that, though it obviously supported him and Johnny and provided Willy's income as well, still wasn't lucrative enough to allow him to afford the important business trip he needed to take without saving up for a full two years. Which led her to assume that finances were an issue for him in a way that finances had never been and would never be an issue for anyone born to the Warwick family.

The Warwick family were all familiar with being asked to invest in any number of things—things like a ranch whose owner wanted to make improvements…

It wasn't a thought Terese wanted to have and she tried to push it out of her mind. But once it was there, it stuck like glue.

If the worst-case scenario were to come about, it wouldn't be the first time someone had wined and dined her to present her with a proposal for their own economic gain.

And yet, merely the idea that that might be what Hunter was about made her feel bad. It certainly took some of the luster off the kiss she'd been reliving since it had happened, some of the luster off the dinner she'd been looking forward to as if it were her first cotillion.

Please don't make that why, she silently implored no one in particular.

But she needed to be mentally and emotionally prepared, she told herself as she stepped out of the shower stall and moved on to applying lotion and powder. She needed to be going into this dinner without any illusions. With her eyes wide open.

And that was what she was determined to do.

Although, even in the midst of trying to brace herself for the possibility that Hunter had something up his sleeve that had nothing to do with being attracted to her, she still kept remembering that kiss.

That kiss had seemed to take him almost as much by surprise as it had her.

That kiss hadn't felt contrived.

That kiss had felt genuine.

And so, so nice…

Maybe she should give him the benefit of the doubt, she thought. After all, Hunter hadn't given her any cause to be suspicious of him. Didn't that mean she could, at least for the time being, take things at face value?

She hoped she wasn't being naive, but she thought she could. If she just didn't go overboard. If she really *did* only think of that kiss as a simple, meaningless kiss, an answer to a momentary impulse and nothing more. If she really *did* think that this dinner was only a way to make amends for the grimy marshmallow and the bad pizza, or that Hunter was merely being polite and entertaining her as a guest who would otherwise be left to her own devices while he went to his meeting at the hospital and Johnny had his evening with Carla and Willy.

Face value. That was the key, she decided. Not making too much of anything that went on between herself and Hunter. Either in the positive or the negative. While still being cautious.

And she *could* be cautious. She could, she vowed as she dressed in the black slacks and black cashmere turtleneck sweater she'd opted to wear. She *could* be cautious and she *would* be cautious.

Except that once she'd brushed out her hair and twisted the ends into a knot that fell between her shoulder blades and judged herself ready to return to the house to begin her evening alone with Hunter, *cautious* was not how she felt.

She felt excited and eager and hopeful. Hopeful that her worst-case scenario wouldn't play out. And that the coming hours would be as good as every other hour she'd spent with Hunter so far.

And that tonight might end with just one more of those simple, meaningless kisses…

Terese didn't mind sitting through the meeting of the Parents Adoption Network. There was some interesting talk about recent problems involving a black-market adoption ring operating out of Russia that members of the Children's Connection were concerned could be connected to their agency and their satellite orphanage in the other country. But so far an investigation had not turned up a link and that news brought with it relief among the PAN members.

The second topic of discussion involved plans for an upcoming bachelor auction that was being held to raise funds. Terese's mind wandered during the first portion of that, but when talk turned to lighthearted attempts to convince the auction chairwoman, Jenny Hall, to bid on a date for herself with someone named Eric Logan, Terese perked up.

"Her face is red but she's smiling so big at that idea that I don't think she's completely opposed to it," Terese leaned over to whisper to Hunter as all eyes went to the pretty chairwoman who was trying desperately to change the subject.

"I think you're right," Hunter whispered back.

"Is Eric Logan related to the woman I met yesterday?"

"Leslie Logan. He's her son," Hunter confirmed. "They're good people. And Jenny is a gem, too. I'd like to see them get together."

The meeting ended soon after that and although they could have stayed for refreshments, Hunter ushered Terese out of the conference room and they went to the restaurant.

The place was crowded. The front portion of it was jammed with people waiting for tables and Hunter left her to weave through the crowd to let the maître d' know they'd arrived for their reservation.

Terese watched him as he did, trying not to devour him with her eyes. But it wasn't an easy task. He was wearing brown tweed slacks, a beige shirt with a brown tie and a cocoa-colored sport coat, and he looked as good in them as he did in his jeans and work shirts.

But she really didn't want to stare so she averted her gaze to a man and woman who were standing at the bar only inches away from her.

The man caught her attention because he had a Portland General Hospital badge clipped to the lapel of his business suit, apparently having forgotten to remove his work identification. Terese was close enough to read his name—Everett Baker—and the word *Accounting*, Children's Connection, underneath it told her what department he was assigned to.

The woman he was with was young and pretty, and wearing a nurse's uniform, so Terese assumed they had just come from work.

She was also too close not to hear what they were talking about—even though she tried not to listen.

Hunter returned just then and caught the eye of the other couple. They exchanged only nods of recognition and vague hellos before Hunter turned his attention to Terese to tell her their table was ready and to lead her through the jam-packed waiting area to the maître d's stand.

It wasn't until they were seated at their table that she said, "Do you know those people at the bar?"

"Not really," Hunter responded. "The woman is a

nurse. Nancy, I think her name is. She was working on Johnny's floor one afternoon when he was at the hospital last week. I was introduced to the man at a fund-raiser once, just in passing. But other than that, no, I can't say that I actually know them."

Terese nodded.

"Do you know them?" Hunter countered as if that possibility had just struck him.

"No, I just noticed his ID badge and since you seem pretty involved with the hospital I thought they might be friends or acquaintances of yours."

"I'm only involved with PAN, not much in the hospital itself."

Terese nodded a second time. But as they opened their menus, something else occurred to her. A way of possibly getting Hunter to show his hand if this dinner was for some purpose other than the meal. And since that worst-case scenario still niggled at her, she decided to do a little test.

So, working to sound nonchalant, she said, "They were talking about a pregnant teenager—that couple from the hospital."

"Were they?"

"Yes," she confirmed. "The nurse was saying it breaks her heart to see how young and alone some the new mothers are. But—it was kind of strange actually—when she said that, the man got so interested it was as if she'd just given him insider-trading tips on a good investment."

Terese had put strong emphasis on that last word

and watched Hunter from under her eyelids without raising her face from the menu to gauge his reaction.

But mention of investments didn't seem to spur anything in him because all he said was, "Maybe it was their first date and he was proving how impressed he could be by what she had to say."

"Maybe," Terese allowed, relaxing slightly because he hadn't taken the bait.

Then he helped her relax even more by changing the subject altogether and referring to the menu.

"The last time I ate here I was with my brother and he had the softshell crab. He said it was the best he'd ever eaten."

"I think I'll try the redfish," Terese countered.

Their waiter brought the wine Hunter had requested then, and after Hunter had ordered for both of them, Terese decided to use the opening he'd given her to make conversation that didn't test him.

"Is the brother you were here with the same brother who was left to help your dad with the ranch when you were in college and your grandfather died?"

Hunter had tasted his wine and he smiled at her as he set the glass down. "You really are a good listener. It must be the psychologist in you," he said in response to the fact that she was referring to what he'd told her the night before.

Then he answered the question she'd worried might have sounded like prying.

"I only have one sibling, so yes, the brother I was

here with is also the one left to help with the ranch. Actually, dinner here was the last time I saw him."

"Did you argue over softshell crab and redfish?" she joked as their salads arrived.

"No, we argued about the ranch. About my refusal to sell it."

"He wanted you to sell the ranch?"

Hunter nodded. "He wanted me to sell it and give him half the money."

"Because he owns half the ranch?"

"Not anymore. I mortgaged the place and bought him out. But originally it was left to the two of us, so when we were here for dinner he still owned half."

"But he didn't want to work it then any more than he wanted to when you were in college?" Terese guessed.

"He's not a *hick* like the rest of us—that's what he said. After my grandfather died, he tried to convince Dad to sell. They had a huge falling out. Sean refused to stick around even though Dad needed the help. But Sean didn't just take off. He cleared out one of the ranch's business accounts first. That was the stuff I said had gone on with him."

Terese raised her brows at that. "He stole from your family?"

Hunter took a deep breath and sighed it out. "Yeah," he admitted, clearly not proud of that fact. "It nearly killed my dad when he realized what Sean had done. Losing the money wasn't as devastating to him as knowing one of his sons had taken it. Dad and Sean never set eyes on each other again."

"Did you have contact with your brother?"

"Not until after Dad died—that was about ten years ago. Sean didn't come to the funeral, but he did contact the estate lawyer to find out if he had anything coming. I thought that took a lot of…guts."

"And your dad had left him half the ranch in spite of everything?"

"Dad struggled with what Sean had done for a long time but he finally decided that if Sean had needed to get away that bad—and had asked him for the money—he would have given it to him. I guess that was his way of forgiving him. But Dad never lost the hope that Sean would change his mind about the ranch and want to come back, want to work it and keep it in the family. I think that's why he didn't take Sean out of his will."

"But even owning half the place didn't make a difference?" Terese asked.

Hunter shrugged and shook his head. "Sean is…I don't know, sort of his own breed, I guess. He always thought he was better. Not only better than us, but better than most people. That he *deserved* better. He said that a lot. The trouble is, he doesn't seem to find anyone who thinks he's quite as good as he thinks he is. So he's hopped from one job to the next, one get-rich-quick scheme to the next, one relationship to the next."

"I take it he hasn't had a lot of financial success and

that's why he wanted you to sell the ranch and give him his half?"

"He started trying to talk me into selling the place as soon as he found out he owned half of it—"

"He couldn't force you to?"

"That was the one thing Dad added to the will—I suppose as a safeguard in case Sean kept on being... Well, Sean. I had the right of refusal to sell. So it was up to me. There was nothing Sean could do without me agreeing."

"That sounds like a recipe for conflict."

"What it meant was that he would come into Portland, put some friendly pressure on me, give me a sob-story about a deal that had gone sour for him, or how much in debt he was, try to convince me of all I was missing in the world by being tied to the ranch— that's how he put it—and why I should sell for both our sakes. I'd refuse, usually give him whatever I could spare to bail him out, and he'd take off again for a year or so before he'd come back and start all over."

Since Hunter didn't seem to mind telling her any of this, Terese prodded, "But the last time...?"

He shrugged again and the expression on his chiseled face reflected sadness. "It got ugly. He said he was sick of this game, sick of having to come around and beg me for handouts when he had a right to half the place. He said he wanted to wash his hands of the ranch, of me, and that was all there was to it. I knew he was never going to change his mind, never going to want to come back, and I finally just gave in. I had the ranch appraised and bought Sean out."

"And you haven't seen him since," Terese said.

"I doubt I'll ever see or hear from him again." The sadness was there in his handsome face again. But apparently Hunter didn't want that to be the tone he set because he tried on a small smile and added, "Unless maybe he ever needs one of my kidneys or something, then he'll probably look me up."

"Families are complicated," Terese confirmed as their salad plates were removed and the main course arrived.

As they settled into enjoying their meals he turned the tables on her. "What about your family and that lesser-twin business? That doesn't sound as if you and your sister are too close."

He'd been open and honest with her and she felt she owed him the same thing, so she said, "We aren't close at all. For twins or even for regular sisters. In fact, it's not altogether unusual for us to go several months without seeing each other—and we live in the same house. Eve is rarely in town. She's usually with friends in Gstaad or London or Paris or, if she's in the country, she's in New York. Portland is home base for her but that mainly just means pit stops."

"I thought all twins were nearly inseparable," Hunter said.

"Well, not us. I guess, like you and your brother, Eve and I have always been very different people. We were never interested in the same things. We never

An Important Message from the Editors

Dear Reader,

Because you've chosen to read one of our fine romance novels, we'd like to say "thank you!" And, as a **special** way to thank you, we've selected <u>two more</u> of the books you love so well **plus** an exciting Mystery Gift to send you — absolutely <u>FREE</u>!

Please enjoy them with our compliments...

Pam Powers

Lift here

Peel off seal and place inside...

How to validate your Editor's
"Thank You"
FREE GIFT

1. Peel off gift seal from front cover. Place it in space provided at right. This automatically entitles you to receive 2 FREE BOOKS and a fabulous mystery gift.

2. Send back this card and you'll get 2 brand-new *Romance* novels. These books have a cover price of $5.99 or more each in the U.S. and $6.99 or more each in Canada, but they are yours to keep absolutely free.

3. There's no catch. You're under no obligation to buy anything. We charge nothing—ZERO—for your first shipment. And you don't have to make any minimum number of purchases— not even one!

4. The fact is, thousands of readers enjoy receiving their books by mail from The Reader Service. They enjoy the convenience of home delivery...they like getting the best new novels at discount prices BEFORE they're available in stores... and they love their Heart to Heart subscriber newsletter featuring author news, horoscopes, recipes, book reviews and much more!

5. We hope that after receiving your free books you'll want to remain a subscriber. But the choice is yours— to continue or cancel, any time at all! So why not take us up on our invitation, with no risk of any kind. You'll be glad you did!

GET A *Free* MYSTERY GIFT...

SURPRISE MYSTERY GIFT COULD BE YOURS **FREE** AS A SPECIAL "THANK YOU" FROM THE EDITORS

DETACH AND MAIL CARD TODAY! ▼

Yes! I have placed my

Editor's "Thank You" seal in the space provided above. Please send me 2 free books and a fabulous mystery gift. I understand I am under no obligation to purchase any books, as explained on the back and on the opposite page.

PLACE
FREE GIFT
SEAL
HERE

393 MDL DVFG   193 MDL DVFF

FIRST NAME	LAST NAME

ADDRESS

APT.#	CITY

STATE/PROV.	ZIP/POSTAL CODE

(PR-R-04)

Thank You!

The Reader Service — Here's How It Works:

Accepting your 2 free books and gift places you under no obligation to buy anything. You may keep the books and gift and return the shipping statement marked "cancel." If you do not cancel, about a month later we'll send you 3 additional books and bill you just $4.74 each in the U.S., or $5.24 each in Canada, plus 25¢ shipping & handling per book and applicable taxes if any.* That's the complete price and — compared to cover prices starting from $5.99 each in the U.S. and $6.99 each in Canada — it's quite a bargain! You may cancel at any time, but if you choose to continue, every month we'll send you 3 more books, which you may either purchase at the discount price or return to us and cancel your subscription.

*Terms and prices subject to change without notice. Sales tax applicable in N.Y. Canadian residents will be charged applicable provincial taxes and GST.

liked the same things. There wasn't a lot we could share. And then my mother died when we were seven—"

"My mother died when I was seven, too," Hunter said with surprise at the coincidence. "She was thrown from a horse."

"My mother was killed in a car accident," Terese offered. "But I haven't heard you mention a stepmother…"

"No, my father never even looked at another woman."

"Well, I can't say that about mine. He was married again almost a year to the day after my mother's death. And his new wife was only twenty-three."

It was Hunter's turn to raise his eyebrows. "Wow."

"Wow is right. She seemed more like someone he would have hired to baby-sit, but all of a sudden she was our mother. Or at least she was Eve's mother."

"Eve's mother? But not yours?" Hunter said to encourage her to explain.

"Ellen—that's my stepmother's name—just took one look at Eve and me and seemed to make up her mind that Eve was going to be her darling and that I was in the way."

"So she was an evil stepmother?"

Terese could tell he was joking so she smiled even though she didn't have a lot of lighthearted feelings about her stepmother.

"Evil might be a little bit of an exaggeration," she said. "But I was definitely not her cup of tea."

"Why not?" he asked as if that were a concept he couldn't grasp.

"In large part it had to do with the fact that Eve was prettier," Terese said matter-of-factly and without self-pity. "For instance, among the many comments in her repertoire, Ellen would say that there were so many things she could do with Eve's hair because it was so fine and silky, but that mine was too coarse and thick and ugly. Or that having Eve was just like having a little china doll to dress up, but that I was all knees and elbows and awkwardness, like a donkey we'd seen in a field."

"Did this woman actually compare the two of you and let you know she thought your sister was better?" Hunter asked in outrage.

Terese mimicked Hunter's earlier shrug. "I don't think a day went by for years and years without Ellen comparing us. And then, as Eve got older and became as obsessed as Ellen had always been with appearances, Eve would chime in, too, about what was wrong with me. But since I didn't want to go through a lot of plastic surgery and—"

"Hold on. The two of them wanted you to have plastic surgery?"

More disbelief. But Terese wasn't sure whether he couldn't fathom that they'd suggested such a thing because it wasn't something she needed or just because it had been insulting.

"Actually they called it surgical *enhancement*," she amended. "To *enhance* my looks so I wouldn't be as plain."

"Plain," he repeated.

"Plain Jane—that's what my stepmother has called me almost since we met. And it caught on. Eve likes to call me that, too. It's almost become my nickname."

Hunter shook his head in disgust. "And that's why you see yourself as the lesser twin."

Terese was sorry she'd ever said that because he seemed to have so much trouble getting past it.

"The Plain Jane thing isn't as bad as it sounds," she assured. "I'm used to it."

"No one should have to be used to being called Plain Jane instead of her own name. Or thinking of herself as being less than anyone else."

"I decided a long time ago to consider the source," she said. "Think of it like this—your brother did something you would never do and certainly you could never respect him for doing, not to mention that you don't respect his lifestyle or the person he is, right?"

"I'd say that's pretty much on the nose, yes."

"Well, I feel the same way about my sister and my stepmother. I wouldn't want to be like either of them any more than you'd want to be like your brother. I wouldn't want appearance to be the focal point of my existence and, although I probably shouldn't say it, it seems shallow to me that that's the case for them. So I consider the source when they put me down, and I don't pay much attention to them."

"I hope that's true. But this sounds as if it's been going on since you were a little girl and I can't imagine that you were considering the source at nine or ten years old. It had to have hurt you and have an impact on you. On your self-image."

"To tell you the truth, the bigger impact came much later and not from my own family," Terese said.

Hunter frowned at that, but after she'd made the comment, Terese decided she didn't want to get into an explanation. So she said, "Let's just say that when it comes to my stepmother and Eve, I survived their opinions of the way I look."

"You survived to call yourself the lesser twin."

Clearly she was making no headway convincing him, so she decided to try making light of it instead. "How do you know I didn't mean that I was the lesser twin because I'm less vain? Or less self-centered? Or less of the things Eve is that I don't want to be?"

That made him smile. "I hope that *is* what you meant. I hate thinking that anyone has convinced you that you're not as good as they are."

"If I guarantee that, will you drop the lesser-twin thing once and for all?" she said more coyly than she'd intended.

"Convince me," he said with a smile that shot heat through her veins.

Terese put her hand to her heart as if she were pledging allegiance and said with flair, "I truly believe I'm the greater twin."

Hunter laughed.

"I'm putting it in my memoirs—under hobbies."

He chuckled and shook his head but the return of their waiter kept him from saying anything.

The waiter tried to tempt them with dessert but neither Terese nor Hunter could eat another bite and they ended up with the bill instead. Hunter insisted the meal was his treat, and once he'd paid, they left the restaurant.

They'd taken Terese's car because Hunter only owned a truck, but he'd driven the sedan and she was content to have him drive it back to the ranch again.

He opened the passenger door for her and advised her to buckle her seatbelt before he locked her in and rounded the front end to the driver's side, slipping behind the wheel.

As they were headed home, he glanced at her, gave her a mysterious sort of smile, and said, "Can I ask you something else about your sister? With the understanding that if you don't want to answer, you don't have to?"

Terese seized the opportunity to look over at him, trying not to dwell too much on the way even the dashboard lights threw the perfect angles of his face into relief.

"Okay," she agreed tentatively.

"We met Eve in the sixth month of her pregnancy and answered any question she asked, but it seemed… indelicate, I guess, to ask her some of what we were curious about."

"Like what?"

"She just seemed like sort of an unusual unwed

mother giving up a baby for adoption—twenty-five, educated, financially able to support a child even without help. It was also hard to believe that she didn't know who the father was, which was what she told us when we asked her that. After last week I feel I should have that information in case anything else with Johnny's health crops up."

They were all reasonable questions. And Terese knew the answers but she debated about giving them.

Would she be out of line if she did?

She wouldn't be betraying any confidences. Eve had somehow seen herself as a victim in it all and she'd talked freely about the entire situation. In fact, Terese had even overheard her sister telling a manicurist all the sordid details. If Eve's manicurist could know, couldn't the man who had ended up as Johnny's dad?

It seemed to Terese that he could.

So she said, "Eve wasn't being evasive when she told you she didn't know who Johnny's father was. She honestly doesn't know because she'd been sleeping with three different men at about the time she got pregnant. One of them was married and she didn't want to approach him with paternity tests because his wife is a friend of hers. One man was a stranger she'd met in Monte Carlo and couldn't track down again. And the third candidate was someone who'd decided he didn't want anything to do with her before she realized she was going to have a baby."

"Oh."

It wasn't a pretty picture and Terese knew it. But she also wasn't certain, now that she'd come this far, if Hunter still wanted to hear more. So, before she continued, she asked him.

"I'm sure," he said.

"Okay. Well, the pregnancy itself was due to a failure in Eve's birth control," Terese explained. "She didn't realize it *had* failed because she was using a long-term method—a shot her doctor gave her every few months that was supposed to keep her from cycling. But apparently it's not the most reliable method of preventing ovulation. When she never cycled, she just thought the shot hadn't worn off and waited another two months before going in to see the doctor again."

"And by then the pregnancy was too far advanced to be terminated," Hunter concluded.

"Exactly. And as for keeping Johnny…" Terese had to pause and steel herself. "Eve never wanted kids and that didn't change just because she was having one. In fact, she had her tubes tied after Johnny was born to make sure this never happened again. And she was adamant about not having Johnny in her life. In any way. It was something I couldn't grasp, but it was also something I couldn't do anything about. There was no talking her into keeping him. Or letting anyone else who was anywhere near her keep him, either."

Hunter took his eyes off the dark country road to look at her again. "You know," he mused, "—and again, I'm not complaining—but there was some hurrying up done at the end of the adoption process that was never explained to us. We thought we were a few days away from getting Johnny and then we got a call from the agency telling us that we had to pick him up within an hour. That wouldn't have had anything to do with you, would it?"

The man was perceptive along with everything else.

But Terese didn't see any reason to lie, so she told him what had gone on immediately after Johnny's birth, that she'd wanted to keep her nephew herself, but that her sister had made sure that didn't happen.

Hunter didn't respond instantly after she'd told him the end of her story. But when he did, his voice was quiet and sympathetic despite what he said. "I can't say I'm sorry she didn't let you have him," he confessed. "But I am sorry that it was so hard on you."

"I'm just glad he got a good home and that I'm getting to know him now," Terese said as they arrived at the ranch.

Hunter bypassed the house to park her car near the cabin. It was late, and since he'd anticipated that they might not be back too early, Willy and Carla were spending the night in the guest room and had apparently already gone to bed, because the only light was the small fluorescent fixture over the sink, which was always left on overnight.

For Terese that meant the evening was coming to an end.

As Hunter turned off the engine, she reminded herself that she'd just had several hours with him and that she had no business regretting that it was over.

But it didn't help.

Hunter got out from behind the wheel and came around to open her door, returning her keys as they headed for the cabin.

But once he'd done that he also did something else along the way that rocked her slightly—he put his hand to the small of her back.

It was probably only a courtesy, she thought, counseling herself not to go to any extremes searching for a reason that that hand was there.

But no amount of counseling could change how much she liked having it there. How nice it felt. Or the fact that it sent tiny electrical charges from that spot outward like brilliant rays of light.

When they reached the cabin, he took his hand away and she did what she'd done on the previous nights—she unlocked the door, reached in to switch on the light, then stepped inside and turned around to face Hunter. All as if she hadn't even noticed that he'd just touched her for the first time.

"After an evening like this I would ordinarily invite you in for a nightcap or a cup of coffee or something," she said, working to sound normal. "But I'm afraid I don't have much to offer in the way of any of that."

"I should be gettin' in anyway," he said with a slow, lazy smile that was so sexy it nearly made Terese's heart stop.

But he didn't make any move to leave. Instead he leaned one shoulder against the doorjamb just as he had on nights gone by. Only tonight he reached out with his other hand and took one of hers.

Like the hand at the small of her back, it seemed a natural enough gesture. It was just that Terese was so taken off guard by it—and so flooded with the thrill of having him touch her again—that she wasn't sure what to do.

But she didn't want him to think she was opposed to any of it so she followed her hand and stepped in a little closer to him than she would have otherwise.

Close enough to smell his aftershave and feel the heat of his big, hard, masculine body...

"Tomorrow it's chores as usual," he said then, apparently unaware that she could barely concentrate on anything except that hand that held hers. "But after dinner tomorrow night I promised Johnny we'd go shoppin' for his Halloween costume. Are you up for that?"

"Sure," she answered feebly.

"And if I finish work with enough time to spare, maybe I'll carve the rest of the pumpkins before dinner."

"Would it help if I cooked?" she heard herself ask while only a small portion of her mind functioned.

The smile on that handsome face she was gazing up at broadened. "That's right," he said as if she'd reminded him of something amusing. "You said you could cook. Maybe I should make you prove it."

"Maybe you should," Terese countered, surprised that her own voice held the same note of intimate teasing that his had.

"Okay, then. I'll carve pumpkins while you cook. But no fair cheatin'," he warned as if he liked the idea that she might.

He was dropping more G's from the ends of his words than he usually did, and it occurred to her that that was part of whatever was going on between them that almost seemed seductive.

And she liked that a little too much, as well.

"How would I cheat at making dinner?" she asked.

"No calls on the sly to the family cook to bring somethin' out here you can claim to have fixed yourself."

"Ah, you just ruined my master plan," she joked.

Hunter leaned forward to confide in a deep voice, "If worse comes to worst, Johnny and I are pretty fond of peanut-butter-and-jelly sandwiches."

"I'll keep that in mind," Terese countered, tilting her face upward in acceptance of the challenge.

Which left their faces very close together.

His topaz eyes met hers then and lingered. Just the way he was lingering in the doorway.

Neither of them said anything. But even without words the air all around them seemed to buzz with a resurgence of that electricity she'd felt when his hand had first settled against the small of her back, electricity that they were somehow generating between them.

And then he came the rest of the way to her to kiss her.

Only, unlike the kiss of the night before, this one was more sure of itself right from the start. His lips parted over hers and urged hers to open beneath them.

He used the hand that held hers to bring her hand to his hip, depositing it there so he could wrap both of his arms around her and brace her head in the palm of one hand as he deepened the kiss even more.

Terese's mind emptied of all thoughts but that kiss and what she was experiencing. What she was relishing. The feel of her hand at his hip. The feel of the honed pectorals beneath her other palm. The feel of his arms around her, of being held close to that masterful body.

His lips parted farther still and the tip of his tongue jutted in only enough to test the very edges of her teeth like a ruddy rebel at the garden gate hoping to attract some company.

Terese's tongue answered the call, tip to tip, timid and brazen at once.

It was all the encouragement he needed. His mouth opened wider over hers and his tongue came boldly in to circle hers, to tease and taunt, to stake a claim as that kiss grew hotter and more sensual by the minute.

Almost too sensual not to inspire thoughts of doing more than kissing. As Hunter's arms wrapped her more tightly and held her so closely to him, she had to slide her hand from his chest around to his back. Her breasts were nearly flattened against him and her nipples kerneled into knots so hard, she wondered if he could feel them nudging insistently into him.

Terese was beginning to notice how many things inside her were coming alive and craving more than kissing—even hot, hungry kissing. Hunter's hands had started a massage of her back that said things might be coming alive in him, too. But just as those messages reached her rational mind, he must have decided it was better not to let this go much further because his tongue did a reluctant retreat and he drew the kiss to a slow, equally as reluctant end.

And then his mouth was gone from hers.

Still, though, he kept his arms around her, remaining where he was as he said, "I hope you weren't too bored at the meeting."

There was never anything boring about the time she spent with him. But she didn't think she should reveal that so she merely said, "I wasn't bored, no." And even if she had been it would all have been worth it for that kiss....

"I had a good time," he added.

"Me, too."

"Thanks for filling in some gaps for me about your sister and Johnny."

"You're welcome. Thanks for dinner," she countered.

Something about that made him smile that deliciously evil half smile again. "You'll make it up to me tomorrow night when you cook, remember?"

Terese smiled back at him. She was going to like proving that she really could cook. "I remember. Do you want the bread on your peanut-butter-and-jelly sandwiches toasted or not?"

Hunter laughed. "Not."

He kissed her once more then. A brief buss.

But even so, he stayed looking into her eyes for a long enough time after that to make her wonder if he might be thinking about kissing her yet again—which would have been very, very all right with her.

In the end, he simply smiled another of those sweetly devilish smiles before he finally let her go.

"I'll see you tomorrow," he said, walking backward from her doorstep.

"Tomorrow," she repeated, secretly wishing they would never run out of them as she leaned against the doorjamb herself to watch him go.

Then he gave her a little wave and spun around on the heels of his cowboy boots to disappear into the mudroom door.

Terese took a last, deep breath of the chilly night air, sighed a happy sigh and then stepped away from the threshold to close her own door.

And that was when it occurred to her that her worst-case scenario had not been played out. Not in any way, shape or form. That, in fact, if she had had a *best*-case scenario, the evening would have been it.

So she'd just been silly to fret about all she'd fretted about earlier, she told her suspicious side victoriously as she kicked off her shoes and headed to the bedroom portion of the cabin.

But as she did she realized something else.

Deep down there was a tiny flicker of hope that the kiss from the previous evening, their dinner tonight and that kiss they'd just shared might mean that Hunter really *did* see something in her that he liked.

And that tiny flicker of hope was enough to scare her to death.

Because where there was that kind of hope, hurt could follow…

Six

"Yoo-hoo! It's me!"

"Come on in. I'm in the kitchen," Terese called when the front door opened without a prior knock or ring of the doorbell and Carla announced herself.

It was just before dinnertime on Thursday evening—the time Carla usually picked up Willy—so Terese had been expecting her.

Carla didn't respond but Terese assumed that she'd been heard because the front door closed and a moment later Carla pushed through the swinging door to join her.

"Willy is out in the barn with Hunter and Johnny," Terese said in greeting. "They're carving pumpkins but they'll be in any minute."

Carla nodded at that information but her interest seemed more on the platter of chicken Terese had set in the center of the table before returning to the stove to clean the mess she'd made.

"Oh boy, that smell just gave me déjà vu," Carla said as she headed for the table.

"Fried chicken?" Terese asked. It had been Johnny's request for the meal she'd agreed to prepare to prove to Hunter that she honestly could cook.

"Fried chicken *here*," Carla qualified. "Funny how a smell can just whisk you back in time, isn't it?"

"To something good, I hope."

"To something bittersweet now that Margee is gone. A picnic Willy and I and Hunter and Johnny and Margee went on the summer before she died. Margee fried chicken for it and that was what the house smelled like when we got here."

"Hunter told me how close you all were," Terese said.

She couldn't help being curious about Hunter's late wife. The fact that Carla had brought her up and there was no one else around seemed as if this might be Terese's chance to do a little fishing.

Carla didn't seem opposed to it. "Margee and I were best friends," she said. "Hunter and Willy were best friends and worked together. So, yes, it just came naturally that the four of us would be about as close as any four people can be without being related by blood."

Carla sat at the table then and began to dig through her purse in search of something.

"Willy said you were having dinner tonight with your parents so you couldn't stay," Terese said, concealing the fact that she hadn't been sorry not to have the company for the meal. "But can I get you something to drink while you wait for him?"

"No, thanks," Carla said. Then she pulled her wallet out of her purse, opened it and went through the clear plastic sleeves that held credit cards and what appeared to be a few photographs.

Carla took out one of the pictures, looked fondly at it herself and then handed it to Terese. "I think this was taken on that same picnic."

Terese was finished cleaning the stove and went to the table to accept the photo, eager to see it. "I wondered what Hunter's wife looked like. There aren't any pictures of her around the house."

"That was the way Margee wanted it. She was a model, you know."

"No, I didn't know."

"Mostly catalog work. But she always said having pictures of herself on display was like bringing her work home with her so she didn't want any out. Besides, even though you wouldn't think it was true of someone who made a living from the way she looked, Margee was the least vain person I ever knew. She always said she didn't want to have to see her face around every corner, that it was the last thing she'd want to decorate with. So all the photographs of her are in albums."

Terese studied the photograph. In it, Carla, Willy

and Hunter's late wife stood side by side, their arms linked.

"Hunter took the picture—that's why he isn't in it—and Johnny was sleeping on a blanket under the tree behind us and we didn't want to disturb him," Carla said.

It didn't matter to Terese because it was only the stunning blonde she was interested in at that moment.

Margee Coltrane had been tall and thin, but still shapely enough to have noticeably perky breasts in the tight, midriff-baring T-shirt she'd been wearing. She'd had sun-streaked blond hair that was shoulder-length and glistened with perfection. And she'd had a face that Terese had no doubt had been in demand—flawless peachy skin, a bone structure the camera loved, heart-shaped lips, gleaming white teeth, a perfect nose and big blue eyes that actually sparkled.

"She was beautiful," Terese said with awe in her tone. Genuine awe. Margee Coltrane had been exquisite. More exquisite than any of Eve's plastic surgeons could ever accomplish.

"I know," Carla said. "And it was all natural, on top of it. She never wore makeup except for a photo shoot; she washed her hair and let it dry on the go and it still looked good. She could eat more than Hunter and Willy put together and never gain a pound. Me, I pack on the weight just thinking about food, and I have to put on makeup and smooth the frizzies in my hair before I go out in public or I might scare small children."

Terese laughed and glanced from the picture to Carla. Carla wasn't classically beautiful the way

Hunter's late wife had been, the way Eve wanted to be, but Carla had her own charm. She had an oval face with full cheeks that dimpled when she smiled, bright green eyes, a turned-up nose and extremely curly hair that she wore cut very close to her head in a style that few people could pull off, but that made her look sporty and carefree.

"Scare small children? You?" Terese said.

"I don't even need a Halloween costume. I just let the circles under my eyes go unconcealed and my hair go unconditioned and that's all it takes."

Terese laughed again. "You are so wrong," she said, meaning it. "I'll bet you could walk into cheerleader tryouts right this minute and win hands-down. You look that young and fresh-faced and adorable."

"Kind lies," Carla said even though she smiled as if the compliment had pleased her. "But I'm no Margee. And I can't even say she just took a good photograph. As good as she looked in pictures, she looked even better in person."

Terese glanced back at the snapshot, not heartened to hear that. "It's sort of demoralizing," she said more to herself than to Carla.

But Carla heard her and gave a wry chuckle. "Tell me about it!" she agreed. "If she hadn't been so nice, I would have hated her!"

That made Terese laugh again. She didn't hate the other woman. But she did suffer a few unpleasant twinges as she studied the image a moment longer. Unpleasant twinges about how any ordinary-looking person could ever compete with someone who had been that beautiful.

Or attract a man who had already had someone that beautiful...

"Here come the boys," Carla said then.

Terese glanced up from the photograph to see through the kitchen window that Hunter, Willy and Johnny were headed for the house.

It seemed to be Carla's cue to get rid of the picture because she reached to take it from Terese. "Let me put this away before the boys see it. I don't want anybody feeling bad."

Terese relinquished the photograph without objection. She was only too glad not to have Hunter see the picture.

Not that she thought he needed it to remind him of his own wife. But she definitely preferred that he not be reminded of just how beautiful that wife had been.

Or, worse yet, glaringly reminded of what Terese believed to be the current reality—that she herself paled miserably in comparison.

Carla stood then and put her purse strap over her shoulder, making it look as if she'd only just arrived.

But even as the men and Johnny came in and greetings and small talk were exchanged before Willy and Carla left, the image of Hunter's late wife haunted Terese.

"Here it is—the pretty princess book! I told you guys I had one," Johnny announced as he climbed into bed that night and waited for Terese to sit beside him on the mattress so she could read his bedtime story.

After the dinner that had received rave reviews from both father and son, Terese, Hunter and Johnny had gone shopping for Johnny's Halloween costume as planned. In the process Johnny had decided that Terese should have a costume, too. That she should be the pretty princess he claimed to have seen in a storybook. The pretty princess he insisted Terese looked exactly like.

Terese had gently rejected the idea of a costume but her nephew hadn't given up until she'd agreed to buy at least a rhinestone tiara that she could wear when she and Hunter took Johnny trick-or-treating.

And now that they were home again and the little boy had had his bath and was ready for bed, he'd dug out the book he'd told them about to show Terese and his father, who sat on the end of the bed.

"See?" Johnny said, opening the book and pointing to the picture of the princess. "You look just like her! She has long hair that she wears in a big braid like yours is now, and blue eyes that twinkle like yours, and some of those dots on her face."

"The dots are called freckles," Terese said, peering over the tiny shoulder at the book.

She didn't see a resemblance between herself and the princess but it pleased her that Johnny thought there was one.

"That's why you have to be the princess for Halloween," Johnny concluded. "You shoulda buyed more than the crown. You shoulda got the whole dress and everything. You woulda been pretty as the princess."

"Okay, enough about the costume," Hunter said. "Just let Terese read the story so you can get to sleep or you'll be too tired for your party or for trick-or-treating tomorrow night."

That was warning enough. Johnny handed the book to Terese. But not without a disclaimer.

"It's really a girls' book. It just came in a box with some other books—*boys'* books. You know, books about cowboys and soldiers and trucks and things. But I threw it out of my toy box once and it opened up when it landed and I remembered the picture and that's how I knew it was you."

"I don't know if this is a book that's *only* for girls," Terese said, putting a fair share of intrigue in her tone. "Usually if there's a pretty princess in a story, there's a handsome prince, too. And princes are boys."

"But do they ride horses and fight bad guys and stuff?"

"Bad guys or ugly monsters, sometimes," Terese said, opening the book to the first page. "We'll just have to see."

The book was more pictures than story so it didn't take long to read. And since there was, indeed, a handsome prince who rescued the princess on horseback from a fire-breathing dragon, Johnny was appeased.

When Terese was finished reading to him, Johnny slipped beneath his covers and said his good-nights to

Terese and his dad as if he were in a hurry to get to sleep so the next day would come quicker.

Terese and Hunter aided that cause by wasting no time leaving the little boy's room to go downstairs.

"You're sure you want to do this?" Hunter asked her along the way. "We can still run by the store before we go to the preschool tomorrow and buy cookies."

"I'm sure," Terese answered as she headed through the living room.

Hunter had only remembered tonight that he'd drawn the honors of providing cookies for the next day's Halloween party. When Terese learned that he intended to buy a package of them to bring, she'd offered to make them instead—tonight after Johnny went to bed. And since Johnny had supported that idea with enthusiasm, because he said the other kids' mothers always brought homemade cookies, Hunter had conceded.

But not without insisting that he help Terese with the chore.

That was just fine with Terese, because even though she'd done a lot of cooking already today, she hadn't done any of it with Hunter as her assistant.

"You're putting in a lot of K.P. duty," Hunter observed as if he were providing another excuse for her to beg off if she wanted to.

"I enjoy it," she assured. "Think of it as my chance to dig in and get dirty."

"Ooo, I like the sound of that," he said in the sexiest tone she'd ever heard.

She knew it was only a teasing innuendo but it still set off little tingles of excitement in her—little tingles of excitement that stayed with her all the way into the kitchen.

"Okay, where do we start?" he asked when they got there.

"We start with rolling up our sleeves and washing our hands," she answered as if he hadn't just turned her thoughts completely away from baking.

Not that baking had made as much of a resurgence in her mind as that suggestion might have indicated. There was actually no reason Hunter couldn't have worked without rolling up the sleeves of his burgundy plaid flannel shirt. But making him roll them up meant that the thick wrists and forearms she found so intriguing would be exposed. Inch by inch. And all while she watched...

Too, while he was at the sink and she was waiting her turn, she couldn't keep from glancing down at his rear end encased in a pair of tight jeans.

She was only human. And besides that bit of sexy insinuation that had just stirred her up, he *had* kissed her until her toes had curled the night before. Kissed her and roused a whole lot of feelings inside her that were still churning around today in spite of her best attempts to get rid of them. Feelings that were obviously brought to the surface again with very little provocation...

"Your turn," Hunter said, interrupting her train of

thought as he dried his hands with a paper towel and moved out of the way.

Terese regained herself in time to yank her gaze up from his derriere and look him in the eye before she replaced him at the sink.

She'd changed clothes after dinner tonight to shed the fried-chicken smell that had infused her shirt and pants. But she hadn't thought she'd end the day baking, and so she'd chosen a white blouse with an embroidered satin strip on either side of the crossover neckline. Despite the fact that it wasn't the best choice for a chef's smock, she didn't want to change again. Besides, the sleeves were only three-quarter length, so she easily pushed them above her elbows.

While she washed her hands, Hunter stood to one side and from the corner of her eye she could tell he was doing a little watching of his own.

He wasn't doing it too openly. His gaze was aimed at his hands as he went on drying them. But Terese could tell he was looking past his hands—right at her rear end hiding behind the blue jeans she wore and the hem of her shirt that fell just to her hipbones. And it occurred to her that their kiss might have had some lingering effects on him, too.

"Okay, so tell me where you learned to cook," Hunter said when Terese had finished washing and drying her hands and had begun to measure the ingredients for oatmeal cookies as Hunter prepared the cookie sheets.

"I was hoping you wouldn't ask me that," she confessed.

"You ran away from home one summer and became a short-order cook to support yourself," he guessed.

"Not quite," she said, wishing it had been that adventurous. "Actually, I think I told you that Eve and I spent the summers in Europe. Our paternal grandmother has lived in Paris most of her life and our father would send us to her as soon as school was out—he said we needed a woman's attention. But Grandmother never knew what to do with us, either. When we were little, she just left us with the au pair, but as we got older, we needed more to keep us busy. More that didn't involve Grandmother."

"You went all the way to Europe to spend the summers with your grandmother but you needed to do things that didn't involve her? Were you okay with that?" Hunter asked.

Terese shrugged. "Was I okay with having absentee parents and grandparents?"

Hunter nodded, his brow creased in a frown that looked disturbed by what he was hearing.

"I really never knew anything else. That was just the way things were. For my sister and I, and for everyone else we knew."

"Other kids from boarding school or kids whose parents ran in the same circles your family did?"

"Right. My father and grandmother—and the families of kids we knew—were just into... Well, themselves and their own interests. They weren't into being hands-on parents or grandparents. That's what nannies were for."

"Nannies and au pairs and boarding schools," Hunter said, his disapproval echoing in his voice.

Terese nodded. She didn't take offense. She'd long ago decided that if she ever had children of her own she wouldn't be the kind of parent her parents and grandparents had been.

"So your grandmother sent you off to summer boarding school to learn to be a cook?" Hunter asked.

In the course of their conversation the first pan of cookies had been put into the oven and the timer went off now to let Terese know they were done.

She took the pan out, put a second one in and returned to the kitchen table where she worked and Hunter was now sitting on one of the chairs watching.

"Eve was easier to engage every summer," Terese went on. "She liked shopping and beauty spas and luncheons and teas. But I got bored with those things fast and I'd ditch her to stay in the kitchen with the cook. When Grandmother realized that was what I was doing, she enrolled me in summer classes at a French cooking school. Not a boarding school, though, just a place where I went during the daytime. Every summer for quite a few years."

"So you're an accomplished chef and you just didn't want to brag," Hunter concluded.

"I don't know how accomplished I am. I rarely get the chance to use what I learned. But I do know how to cook."

"And you have a skill you could fall back on if bad times ever hit the Warwick clan. I can just see it—you in the kitchen and Eve waiting tables at the Warwick All-You-Can-Eat Buffet."

Terese laughed out loud. "Or maybe we'd call it Warwick's Wieners and Wings, and I'd hire Johnny to roast marshmallows for dessert."

"No extra charge for dropping them on the ground on the way to the table," Hunter contributed, laughing along with her.

Then he said, "Well, regardless of where you learned or why, the fried chicken tonight was the best I've ever had and I really appreciate you making cookies for Johnny's party. Sometimes I'm not so good at being dad *and* mom."

To Terese that seemed like her second opportunity of the day to bring up the subject of his wife, to maybe get him to continue what Carla had begun and tell her about the woman who had mothered Johnny for the first two years of his life.

But for a moment Terese was torn between her own nagging curiosity and that thought she'd had earlier about not wanting Hunter to be reminded of his late wife. His *beautiful* late wife.

Only now the nagging curiosity got the better of her and she couldn't pass up what felt like an open door.

Keeping her gaze intently on the cookie dough she was dropping from an ice cream scoop onto the other sheet, she said, "Carla said your wife made good fried chicken."

"She did," Hunter answered. He didn't offer more than that, though, and Terese wasn't sure if she should persist or not.

She decided to give it one more try.

"Carla said the smell in the house today gave her déjà vu. Did it do that to you, too? Did it bring back memories of your wife?"

"A lot of things do, but the smell of fried chicken today didn't, no," he said, stopping there as if that was the end of the conversation.

Okay, so maybe he didn't want to talk about his wife. Terese decided she wouldn't push it.

But then, just when she thought Hunter wasn't going to say more, he did.

"So Carla flashed back on Margee, huh?"

"She said she did. To a picnic you all went on."

Hunter nodded. "We had some good times together," he said. There was nostalgia in his tone but not sadness, so Terese amended her decision not to push the subject of his wife and said, "You and Willy were best friends and Carla and your wife were best friends, Carla said."

"True."

"So how did the two couples come about? Was Willy dating Carla and they introduced you to your wife, or what?"

"There wasn't really any introducing, no. We all went to the same high school, the one in the suburb nearest to here, where Carla and Willy still live and where we'll take Johnny trick-or-treating tomorrow night. Willy and I were friends from the fifth grade, when his family moved to Oregon. Carla was in our sixth grade class and even then Willy did a lot of showing off for her in spite of swearing that he didn't like her. Then Margee came in the ninth grade. She moved in next door to Carla the summer before and they became fast friends."

"Were Carla and Willy dating already in the eighth grade?"

"No, it was still more of him watching her from afar. They didn't start what you'd call dating until we were sophomores, and by then I kind of had my eye on Margee. We'd had a couple of classes together, passed each other in the hall, that kind of thing."

"Did Carla and Willy have anything to do with you getting together with her?"

"They encouraged it, the way kids do. They thought I should ask her to the homecoming dance."

"Did you?" Terese inquired as she took another sheet of cookies out of the oven and put one more in.

"I did. And she said no."

Terese laughed. "Uh-oh."

"I'd waited too long and she already had a date. But I took her to the movies the week after homecoming."

"And you were together from then on?"

"Pretty much. She left for a while to pursue the modeling thing. That's what she did."

"Carla told me."

"But once she was getting fairly regular work and was established with an agency, she came back here and we got married three weeks before Willy and Carla did."

"How long ago was that?"

"Eight—almost nine—years."

"So you'd only been married about three years when you decided to adopt a baby? I mean, I know it takes some time for the paperwork and everything, and Johnny is four…"

"Actually Margee wanted kids right away. But she had an ectopic pregnancy early on that did some damage and after that she just couldn't seem to conceive again. That was why we went the adoption route. And it was two years after we filed the initial paperwork before we got Johnny."

"And only another two years before you lost her," Terese said quietly.

Hunter nodded and this time there was an air of sadness to it. "She was on her way to shoot a swimsuit catalog in California. It was a remote shoot, she had to take a helicopter to the location, and the helicopter went down. There were no survivors."

"You must have been devastated."

"I don't even remember those first few months. I think I was a zombie. I just got up in the morning, put one foot in front of the other, and did whatever I could to get through the day. Willy and Carla stayed close and filled in whatever gaps I left."

"What about Johnny? How much of it could he grasp at two?"

"Not much. He just kept asking for her. Crying for her. There was no way to make him understand what had happened. I tried, but he was just too small. All I could do was keep saying that his mom was gone, that she couldn't come back. Eventually he gave up."

"Having him ask for her, cry for her, must have made it even harder on you," Terese said, her own voice cracking with sympathy.

"Broke my heart all over again every time. But we got through it," Hunter added on a note of resignation and resiliency.

"And since then?" Terese asked, unable to restrain her curiosity. "Have you dated at all?"

Hunter laughed a wry laugh. "Nope."

"You must have had the chance," Terese persisted.

"Doesn't matter. Once I got my head above water after Margee's death, I sorted through where I thought my life and Johnny's should go. Of course I thought about dating. But it just seemed like Johnny should be my central focus, that anyone else I brought into the mix would detract from the attention he needed, the attention I wanted to give him. So I put a moratorium on getting involved with anyone and that meant no dating."

Terese wondered how her being there and what they were doing—whatever it was they were doing—fit into that. But she didn't ask. Instead, she said, "What about now? Does Johnny talk about his mother?"

Hunter didn't seem to think it odd that she'd veered from the topic of dating and merely answered her question. "He talks about her some, here and there. But not all that much. He understands that she died, although I'm not sure what his concept of that is. I think it's more that he just doesn't have much memory of her so she doesn't seem real to him."

"Does he not remember her at all?" Terese asked, removing another pan of cookies from the oven when the timer went off and putting in the last sheet.

"He seems to have some vague memories, but that's about it. It's too bad, too, because Margee was a great mom and she loved Johnny like nothing I've ever seen. She was just a great person all the way around. She was warm and sweet and kind and generous and patient and giving and..."

When he paused suddenly Terese stopped putting cooled cookies into the cookie tin where she was stacking them and glanced at him, worried that he was too upset to continue.

But that wasn't the case. Instead she saw Hunter looking at her as if he'd just renewed his focus on her.

Then he said, "There were a lot of things about Margee that aren't unlike you, now that I think about it."

"Me?" Terese parroted in amazement. "I'm a long way from being a model."

Hunter ignored that. "Margee was someone who had a lot more going for her than her looks. And she took it all for granted. She was oblivious to what made her really special."

And he thinks I'm like that? Special? Terese thought in amazement.

That possibility flattered and embarrassed her at the same time and she could feel her cheeks turning red.

"Let me get this mess cleaned up," she muttered and took the empty bowl to the sink.

Hunter must have seen the blush and she was grateful that he gave her a few minutes to regroup. He stacked more of the cookies in the tin, while she rinsed the dishes and utensils and put them in the dishwasher.

The timer rang and she took that last sheet of cookies out of the oven, continuing to keep herself occupied while she dealt with what he'd said and the effect it had on her.

The effect *he* had on her—not only with his words, but also with those eyes that followed her.

Those eyes that emanated such warmth that, despite the fact that they'd just been talking about his wife, Terese began to believe Hunter actually did see her in her own light. That he did see her as special.

It wasn't until she was rinsing the sink that he finally stood and joined her. When he did, he didn't just come to stand beside her. He turned his back to the counter and partially insinuated himself in front of her, facing her so he could peer down into her eyes.

"Are you done being embarrassed?" he asked, in a voice that was low, gentle, quiet. And very intimate.

Terese managed a small smile. "Not quite," she said, only half joking.

Hunter laid his forehead against hers. "I'd like to

erase every not-nice thing anyone has ever said to you," he whispered. "And convince you how terrific you are."

Terese couldn't help smiling, and blushing, all over again.

But this time Hunter didn't give her any space in which to suffer her discomfort. This time he stayed where he was, studying her, smiling affectionately.

Then he kissed her forehead, lingering and letting the heat of his breath bathe her skin for a moment. Long enough for her to forget all about being embarrassed. To forget all about how his late wife had looked. To forget about everything but how good it was to have him there.

He abandoned her brow then and brought a single finger to curve under her chin, to tip it up so he could press his mouth to hers.

That initial kiss was very tender. But the one that followed was deeper. More serious. He slid his hand from under her chin to cup the back of her head, to brush tiny strokes of his thumb up into her hair.

With a will of their own, her arms went around him and Terese pressed her palms to his shoulder blades while their lips met and separated and met again. Deliberately. Lazily. Leisurely.

At least it was deliberate and lazy and leisurely for a time. Until that was all replaced with a stronger need, a hunger that grew steadily, making those kisses more intense, more demanding.

Hunter moved completely between her and the

counter, taking her fully into his arms, holding her tightly against his long, lean length and turning her so that their positions were reversed and it was Terese whose back was to the counter's edge as his mouth opened wide over hers and his tongue came to plunder and please.

Then he slid his hands down her sides, to her hips and back again, stopping at her waist where he tightened his grip and lifted her to sit on the countertop so they were at equal heights. Her legs straddled him when he finessed them apart so he could step into their V.

Terese had a fleeting thought of decorum—or the lack of it in that position—but it was only fleeting, chased away by too many other, better thoughts. And feelings. And sensations.

Once again her hands had a will of their own and they coursed from his back to his sides and up his front, ending at honed pectorals. It was a path she longed for his hands to take on her body, to satisfy the nipples that were kerneled and straining for notice.

Hunter pulled her slightly forward, balanced on the edge of the countertop where he urged her to wrap her legs around him, to hook her ankles behind his waist as his kisses grew more frenzied.

Terese's fingers and flattened palms were in Hunter's hair one minute, tracing the breadth of his shoulders the next, the narrowing V of his back the minute after that. She just couldn't get her fill of the feel of that hard body that ranch work had perfected, so, without thinking about anything but the pure desire to be free of interference, she pulled his shirt tails from his jeans.

No sooner had she slipped her hands underneath to the satin over steel of his naked back than Hunter took her lead and reached under the hem of her own shirt.

Warm, strong, intriguingly callused hands pressed against her flesh and sent tiny shards of sparkling promise all through her, promise of more as he massaged and kneaded her back.

Terese arched her spine and let those tiny knots of desire that were her nipples meet Hunter's chest, hinting at needs she wasn't sure he understood.

But apparently he did, because while one hand braced her from behind, the other finally answered that need by covering her breast.

The only flaw was the bra she wore. Even that scant bit of lace was too much of a barrier and she was so, so happy when Hunter reached inside the cup to take that engorged globe into his palm.

His mouth left hers then to kiss her neck, from a sensitive spot right below her earlobe all the way to her collarbone. Kissing. Nibbling. Flicking the tip of his tongue here and there and leaving little damp spots to air dry and send chills of delight dancing along the surface of her skin.

Then he kissed another path to the hollow of her throat, all the while kneading her breast, rolling her nipple between gentle fingertips, lightly pinching and pulling and driving her level of need even higher.

So high she began to fantasize about clothes being shed. About unbuttoning Hunter's shirt. About slipping it off those massive shoulders. About baring his chest to her gaze, to her hands, to her mouth. About unfastening his belt buckle, his waistband button, his zipper…

But that was when her old familiar self-doubts chose to rear their ugly head again, warning her that if she threw off Hunter's clothes the way she wanted to, her own would follow. That not only would he be left bare for her to see, but that she would be left exposed to him, too.

And she didn't think she could do that.

Not when they'd just spent so much time talking about his wife.

His *beautiful* wife.

"Wait," she said suddenly, when she felt him reach to unfasten her bra.

He stopped instantly, resting his hands on either side of her waist instead. Hands that felt so fantastic she wanted them moving all over her, not stalled and still.

But now that her own lack of self-esteem had asserted itself once again, the feeling was every bit as powerful as her desires for him. Maybe more powerful because it took control.

"I think we'd better slow this down," she said.

She couldn't look into his astonishingly handsome face and resist him, so she aimed her gaze much lower, bowing her head, and Hunter dropped his forehead to the top of it.

"Just when I was lookin' to speed it up?" he countered with a teasing, cajoling tone.

"*Especially* when you're lookin' to speed it up," she said, echoing him.

She sensed more than saw his smile as her eyes took in the sight of his narrow hips, his long legs and thick thighs—that body hers was yearning for yet.

But she held fast to her resolve and made up a laundry list of excuses. "Johnny's just upstairs, and we're in the kitchen, and tomorrow is a big day, and—"

"And you're feelin' a little scared and self-conscious," he added, letting her know he knew the truth.

"A little," she confirmed in a soft voice.

He kissed the top of her head and left his lips resting there a while before he finally conceded and pulled his hands out from under her shirt.

Then he raised his head, took a step backward and, touching her only on the outside of her clothes, lifted her off the counter to stand in front of him.

Then, with a resigned and reluctant sigh he said, "Come on, we better get you out of here before I decide to persuade you otherwise."

He took her hand in his then and led her through the mudroom and outside to the cabin.

And the whole way Terese had to fight the regret that he'd done exactly what she'd asked him to do.

When they reached her door, she opened it and, following the same pattern from every other night, she stepped inside and turned back to face him where he stood in the doorway.

Only tonight he didn't hesitate to reach a hand to her face, brushing her cheek with his fingertips and making her nearly shiver with wanting so much more than that.

"Okay, there you are. Delivered safe and sound," he said, his topaz eyes searching hers, his supple mouth curved into an indulgent smile.

"Thank you," she said, not feeling a single ounce of gratitude as the longing to be in his arms, to be doing again what they'd been doing moments before surged within her to almost unbearable levels.

As if he knew it, he said, "You're sure?"

She wasn't. How could she be when she wanted him so much?

But still she repeated some of her excuses, "Johnny, Halloween…"

"You're afraid."

Terese smiled and very nearly gave in.

But in the end she didn't.

Instead she said, "I'll see you in the morning."

He sighed and chuckled. "In the morning," he said.

Then his hand cupped the side of her face and he leaned forward and kissed her again, sending his tongue for one final taste of what she was missing. Then he stopped, pulled his hand away and said, "Good night, Pretty Princess."

That made her laugh just a little. But all she said was, "Good night."

She had to fight the inclination to reach out and stop him when he finally stepped away from the threshold, but she managed to force herself to move farther inside and shut the door rather than watch him go all the way to the house tonight.

Even without that last look at him he stayed vividly in her thoughts, in her mind's eye.

In her blood...

Making it run hot and wild through her veins with all he'd just aroused in her.

All she wished she'd had the courage to let him soothe and satisfy...

Seven

Since Hunter was leaving for Europe on Saturday, he needed time Friday morning to pack. While he did that, Willy worked the ranch alone, and Terese made an artichoke casserole to contribute to dinner at Willy and Carla's before taking Johnny trick-or-treating in their suburban neighborhood.

Johnny was keeping his dad company in Hunter's bedroom. The four-year-old was already dressed in his superhero costume even though the party at his preschool wasn't until that afternoon. He was sitting cross-legged at the head of the bed, bouncing slightly because he was too excited to sit still.

Despite that, Hunter decided to seize the opportunity to talk to the little boy. "So you're okay with

Terese staying here with you while I'm gone, right?" Hunter asked his son as he brought shoes from the closet, wrapped them and placed them in the suitcase.

"Uh-huh," Johnny confirmed.

"Will you be all right with her taking you to the doctor next week?"

"No needles!" the child warned.

"No needles," Hunter assured. "Not for you, anyway. Terese has to have some blood taken, but you don't. The doctor just wants to take a look at you and make sure you're doing well, that you don't have bruising or anything to worry about."

"Okay, then. I'll go and I'll hold T'rese's hand when they take her blood."

Hunter smiled at his son's bravery when it came to someone other than himself being stuck.

"I'm sure that will help," he said. Then he got back to the subject they'd veered from. "You know that Willy and Carla will still be watching you, too. Willy will be here every day just like always."

"I know it."

"And you'll still need to do your chores without being told and to lend Willy a hand if he needs it."

"Uh-huh."

"And Carla will come in every morning when she brings Willy to work and every night when she picks him up. Plus you'll probably all have dinner together some nights or you might stay with Carla and Willy or they might stay here if Terese needs to go somewhere."

"Where would T'rese need to go?" Johnny demanded as if that were unfathomable.

"I don't know. I'm just saying if something should come up and she needs to go somewhere—"

"Without me?" That was more unfathomable yet.

"Yes, without you. I don't think that will happen, but if it does, you'll stay with Willy and Carla."

"Okay," Johnny said, sounding as if that were too farfetched for him to waste any more thought on. Instead he began bouncing even more.

Hunter paused for a moment after tossing rolled-up socks into the suitcase. "Are you paying attention to what I'm saying here, big guy? Or are you just thinkin' about Halloween?"

The little boy shook his head rapidly. "I'm payin' 'tention. T'rese is watchin' me, and Willy and Carla will be here like usual."

"Right. But if you don't want Terese to stay with you and you'd rather go back to our original plan and just stay with Willy and Carla—"

"No, I like this new plan. I like T'rese."

Hunter had been worried that as the day of his actual leaving neared, Johnny might have second thoughts or insecurities about being looked after by someone he hadn't known very long. But that didn't seem to be the case.

"You really do like Terese, don't you?" Hunter said.

"Uh-huh," Johnny said. "She's nice and fun and she smells good. Not like the cracks in the sidewalk."

Hunter laughed. "Terese doesn't smell like the cracks in the sidewalk?"

"No. She smells good."

"How do you know what cracks in a sidewalk smell like and who *does* smell that way?"

"I smelt them once. Me and Mikey did it at recess one day. And the janitor lady smelt just like that when she comed in to clean the mess Michael J.'s hamster made when we letted it out of the cage and it got scared."

"I see," Hunter said, silently agreeing with his son that Terese *did* smell good even though he couldn't compare the light, clean, flowery scent of her to either sidewalk cracks or the preschool janitor.

"Do *you* like T'rese?" Johnny asked then.

"I do," Hunter said, without having to think about it first because it was a thought that was on his mind a lot lately. He did, indeed, like Terese. A lot. Maybe more than he should.

"Does that mean we can keep her?"

Hunter stopped midway through folding a shirt. "Can we keep her?" he repeated.

"Yeah, you know, like when you come back from your trip and stuff, can we keep havin' T'rese here?"

"Well, no," Hunter said, surprised by the question and not quite sure how to answer it. "Terese isn't a pet, you know."

"I know. She's a *lady*," Johnny said, putting a silly inflection on the word. "But she could stay here and play with me and read to me and make more cookies and chicken and smashed potatoes, couldn't she?"

"Well, no," Hunter repeated. "She's just here visiting, like when Great-Aunt Rose comes to stay with us for a while."

"Great-Aunt Rose smells funny, too. Not like the cracks in the sidewalk, but funny."

Hunter refrained from explaining that his late wife's aunt reeked of mothballs and instead continued to make his point. "Great-Aunt Rose lives somewhere else and so does Terese. Terese has a job, and other people she knows and needs to see, and other things she has to do. She can't just stay here to play with you and make you fried chicken. She's only spending some time with us."

That *us* rang in Hunter's ears. Terese wasn't there to spend time with them both; she was there to spend time with Johnny. But somehow, Hunter realized, he seemed to have lost sight of that.

Remembering it now, though, didn't change the fact that he was enjoying having her there as much as his son was.

Which was also probably something that shouldn't be true...

"Does that mean that when you come back from your trip T'rese will go away and we won't see her again?" Johnny asked, frowning fiercely at that possibility.

"No," Hunter said. But this *no* didn't come out as quickly or as confidently as the others had because it occurred to him that he didn't know what would happen with Terese when he got back.

"Will she come and stay with us again?"

"I don't know," Hunter said honestly.

"Will she just come over sometimes, like Carla and Willy do?"

"Maybe," Hunter said, wondering why it was that Johnny's suggestion that they might not see Terese again when he returned from his trip had caused his gut to clench.

He tried to ignore it and went on with what he'd been about to say. "But Terese doesn't live as close to us as Willy and Carla so it won't be as easy for her to drop in like they do."

That fact didn't sit well, either. After having her with them or, rather, right outside their back door, it seemed unpleasantly odd to think of her all the way on the other side of Portland again.

"I think she should just live in the cabin forever," Johnny concluded. "I'll keep makin' her pi'tures to put up because she loves 'em and says they're words of art—"

"You mean *works* of art," Hunter corrected.

Johnny ignored the correction. "—and then she'll like that that's her house and she'll stay."

You wouldn't think that if you knew where she came from, Hunter thought, remembering suddenly that there were vast differences between where Terese had come from and where he was, vast differences between his life and Terese's life, vast differences in where they would go from here.

But he didn't want to think about that right then. He

was leaving in less than twenty-four hours. He'd be gone for a full two weeks. And something as weighty as his relationship with Terese was more than he could deal with at that moment.

"Let's just concentrate on today and tonight and the trip for now, okay?" he told his son.

And that was exactly what he intended to do.

Although, despite how big and important the trip was, it still didn't manage to be uppermost in his mind.

Today and tonight were what kept creeping into his thoughts even when he was packing his bags.

Today with Johnny and Terese for Johnny's party.

Tonight with Johnny and Terese and Willy and Carla for dinner and trick-or-treating.

Later tonight, after Johnny was in bed, when he'd have time alone with Terese.

Oh, yeah, that was definitely a better thought than where Terese had come from or where they'd go from here.

"But how can you be the Pretty Princess if you don't wear the crown?" Johnny reasoned as Hunter parked in the preschool parking lot that afternoon.

As they'd pulled into the lot, Terese had removed the rhinestone tiara she'd been wearing all day to please her nephew. She didn't want to wear the rhinestone tiara into the school.

"I'll be the Pretty Princess again *after* the party," she countered.

"But it's a Halloween party," Johnny pointed out, turning *Halloween* into a singsong.

"But it's a Halloween party for the kids, not for the adults," Hunter contributed as he stopped the engine.

"I promise that as soon as we leave I'll put the crown back on and I won't take it off again the whole rest of the day," Terese added while they all unfastened their seatbelts and got out.

"Okay," Johnny finally conceded with a hint of a pout.

The pout didn't last long, though, because he spotted his friend just then, shouted, "Mikey!" and darted off.

"Be careful of cars!" Hunter called after him.

But Johnny had already safely reached his friend and his friend's mother to walk with them through the parking lot.

As Terese and Hunter followed behind, Hunter leaned slightly toward her and said, "You're sure patient with him."

"Are you kidding? He thinks I look like a fairy-tale princess and he wants to include me in his next-to-the-bestest-holiday—"

"The bestest being Christmas," Hunter supplied what Johnny hadn't left out any of the times he'd told them that today.

"I'm flattered and thrilled," Terese finished.

Hunter studied her for a moment as if he were marveling at something. Then he said, "You really are, aren't you? Thrilled, I mean, that he wants you in on his second-bestest holiday? Even if it means he nags you and wants you walking around in public wearing a tiara?"

"I really am," she said. "I take it as a sign that he likes me and that's nice."

"Oh, he likes you, all right," Hunter said as if he knew something she didn't.

But Terese couldn't question him about it because someone called his name from a distance and drew his attention.

Terese watched him wave at the person—another father—exchanging some private joke about a meeting at the hardware store. She didn't know what they were kiddingly yelling back and forth about but, then again, she wasn't trying to understand it either. She was too lost in trying not to be obvious about the fact that she was ogling him.

He'd gone for a haircut right after lunch and although his hair was still not extremely short, the dark blond mass had been trimmed to fall in a slightly more controlled disarray that made him look neat enough but still natural and untamed.

He was dressed in a heavy mustard-colored flannel shirt that brought out the specks of brilliant gold in his eyes, and she couldn't help wondering if it was as soft as it looked. She also couldn't help the itch she had to test that softness for herself. Or to test the hardness of the muscles the shirt barely contained.

With the shirt, he had on a pair of blue jeans that were tighter than those he usually wore, tight enough to encase his derriere and thick thighs in a way that left no doubt his was a body to be reckoned with. She was left wondering much too much what that body would look like *without* the hip-hugging jeans…

"Shall we go in?"

It was Hunter's voice that pulled her out of her thoughts, and Terese realized suddenly that she'd been caught staring at him. She jolted out of her reverie, hoping it would seem more that she'd been day-dreaming than that she'd been scrutinizing him, and said, "Whenever you're ready."

He didn't make any other comment so she could only hope she'd managed to fool him.

When they went inside, the school lobby was full of costumed children and their parents. Johnny rejoined them then, his freckled face alight with excitement.

"You guys are s'posed to go to the cafeteria and I'm s'posed to go to my room. Then we'll come in and do our parade for you. So me and Mikey are goin', okay?"

"Okay," Hunter said. But he didn't move from that spot until he'd watched his son actually go through the doorway into his classroom.

Then Hunter pointed out the cafeteria and he and Terese did as Johnny had told them to.

In the cafeteria the grown-ups lined the walls, leaving the center free for the costume parade that would kick off the party.

It wasn't long before the preschool teacher came in, hit a button on a boom box to start marching music and the kids filed in, circling the room so everyone could see every costume.

The kids were all in high spirits, many of them preening and showing off and acting like whatever character they were dressed as.

Terese thought they were all adorable. The pure joy and innocence of a whole bunch of costumed four-year-olds was something she'd never experienced before and she delighted in watching the display almost as much as the kids delighted in their celebration.

After the parade there were games—some that the adults could participate in and others that they merely watched—and then refreshments were served.

Through it all, Terese was mistaken several times for Hunter's wife and Johnny's mother. It was an honest mistake since she was there with Johnny's father. And since there were several times when Hunter leaned close to her ear to speak to her without being overheard, or guided her to a new spot with a familiar hand at the small of her back, or touched her arm or her shoulder or her hand.

Sometimes it seemed slightly awkward to explain to a parent that she was merely a friend of the family, but beyond that Terese had no complaints. Not when the nearness of Hunter and the attention he was paying her sent secret thrills coursing through her, reminding her of what had begun in his kitchen the night before.

And she wondered all over again if she should have seized the moment when she had the chance. She wondered if they had been a moment, a chance, she might never have again.

After the Halloween party, Terese, Hunter and Johnny went to Willy and Carla's house, a small, single-story white clapboard that looked as if it had been built soon after the Second World War, when housing was needed for returning soldiers and their brides.

The inside, decorated with numerous handmade crafts and country pine furniture upholstered in blue and brown plaid, was so welcoming that Terese felt right at home the minute she went in the front door.

Dinner was simple. Terese's artichoke casserole went with roast beef, potatoes and gravy, salad and rolls. Terese was the only one at the table wearing a tiara, but Johnny was happy again and that was all that counted.

After the meal Hunter and Terese took the boy door to door. The weather had cooperated and although the temperature was chilly, there was no wind and the rapid walking to follow Johnny, who ran the entire time, kept them warm.

The little boy would have gone on forever, so Hunter had to be firm to get him back to Willy and Carla's house where the pillowcase Johnny had used to collect his goodies was dumped out onto the kitchen table to be inspected before Johnny could have any of it.

But while the adults were sorting through Johnny's loot, Johnny disappeared.

"Where'd he go?" Hunter asked when he noticed his son was no longer there. "I thought he couldn't wait to eat some of this."

"He went to the bathroom, but that was a little while ago," Carla said, getting up from the kitchen table to search.

A moment later she called for them in a hushed voice, and when Terese, Hunter and Willy followed the sound, they found Johnny in the guest bedroom, curled up on the bed, costume and all, sound asleep.

"Looks like he finally had enough Halloween," Terese whispered.

"We'd better get him home," Hunter said.

"Nah," Willy contributed. "Why don't you let him sleep? We have a change of clothes for him from the last time he stayed overnight and I'll bring him with me when I pick you up for the airport. You can say goodbye to him then."

Hunter glanced back at his sleeping son and seemed to consider the suggestion before he said, "You don't care if you have an impromptu overnight guest?"

"You know we don't," Carla confirmed. "Let him sleep."

Hunter shrugged. "Okay, if you're sure."

That seemed to put an end to the evening, though, and after Johnny's candy was replaced in the pillowcase, good-nights were said all around and Terese and Hunter left. Alone.

But Terese didn't want to think about that.

Or about how things changed without Johnny.

As if talking about him would still add some chaperoning benefits, once they were headed home she said, "Poor Johnny. After all day of waiting for his candy, he zonked out before he even got one caramel."

Hunter chuckled. "Don't worry, he'll make up for it. You'll have to hide it and dole it out a piece or two a day while I'm gone or he'll eat a ton at a time and be bouncing off the walls."

While he was gone...

For some reason it only sank into Terese's mind right then that in just a few hours Hunter was leaving. She wouldn't see him for a full two weeks.

The realization deflated her spirits considerably, even if she *would* still be with Johnny.

"I won't tell if you want to ditch the crown now," Hunter said then, once again pulling her out of her thoughts. Thoughts that weren't nearly as pleasant as the ones she'd been having earlier in the day about how terrific he looked.

She reached up and removed the crown that she'd been wearing for so long she'd forgotten about it, smoothing her hair in place and hooking it behind her ears. Johnny had also decreed that she wear her hair loose and flowing the way the princess in the book sometimes had, but she didn't like it falling in her face.

"So, did you have a good Halloween?" Hunter asked then, as if it were a bigger holiday than it was.

"The bestest ever," Terese answered, playing along and trying to stave off the odd sinking feeling brought on by the reminder that he was leaving.

Clearly Terese's somber mood wasn't something Hunter was aware of; his train of thought remained on Halloween. "How do you usually spend it?"

Terese laughed. "Like any other day. College students keep it out of the classroom, and at home… Well, trick-or-treaters don't come through the gates and hike up the mile-and-a-half drive to the house to ring the bell."

"No big society Halloween parties at the country club or anything?"

"Not as a rule. I know people who have them for their kids, but I don't get invited to those."

Hunter took his eyes off the road to glance at her. "You know, there's something you said a couple of days ago that I keep wondering about."

"And it has to do with Halloween and kids' parties?"

"No, with kids in general, though. And today, watching how much fun you were having with Johnny, I've really been wondering about it."

"What is it?" she asked.

"When you made your appointment to be tested for the hemophilia gene, you said you didn't think it would matter because you probably won't ever get married or have a family."

"Ah…"

"I keep wondering why you would think a thing like that."

Terese shrugged. "Past experience," she said simply.

"What kind of past experience could lead you to think you'll never marry and have kids?"

Terese weighed whether to get into this subject with him. It wasn't something she'd ever told anyone outside her immediate family. It had just been too humiliating, too degrading, to talk about.

But somehow the thought of telling Hunter didn't seem so insurmountably embarrassing.

She looked over at him, at his impeccable profile, and warned, "This is my deepest, darkest secret."

"It is?" he said, tossing her a confused frown.

"It is."

"I'm pretty good with secrets," he assured. But he didn't push it, leaving her free to either confide in him or refuse to.

Except that the more Terese considered confiding in him, the more comfortable she felt with it. Especially sitting in the dark cab of his truck, not having to look him in the eye when she did.

"I was engaged once," she said, taking the leap. "To a history professor. It was five years ago. We met at a faculty meeting. His name was Dean Wittiker. He got teased a lot about what he'd be called if he became the dean of the college—he'd be Dean Dean Wittiker." She'd tried to lighten the tone by repeating the joke but somehow it fell flat.

"And you and Dean Dean Wittiker hit it off?"

"We did. Or at least I thought we did. I was a little leery when he asked me out because he was an extremely good-looking guy. Half the coeds had crushes on him and a few actually followed him around campus like little sheep. It didn't seem logical that someone who could have the most beautiful women in the world would be interested in me."

Hunter sighed exaggeratedly. "No Terese-bashing," he ordered.

She laughed a little. "Just reporting the facts," she countered.

"So you went out with him," Hunter said, reminding her where she'd left off so she would go on.

"I turned him down a few times but he was persistent and I finally said yes. We went to dinner and it was nice. There were no lulls in the conversation, we liked the same foods, the same movies, the same books, the same television programs… We *seemed* to have a whole lot in common."

"You *seemed* to have a whole lot in common? What does that mean?"

"It means that after it was over I was left not quite sure what had been real and what had just been part of the ploy to reel me in."

"Like a fish?"

"Like the *big* fish," Terese said quietly because that particular phrase touched on one of the sorest spots.

"Anyway," she continued. "We dated for about six months and *seemed* to be getting closer and closer, and, well, I fell in love with him. He said he loved me, too, and for a while I honestly thought I'd met my soulmate." She couldn't help the cynicism that echoed in that word. "Then he proposed and I accepted, thinking that right there, kneeling in front of me, were all my dreams come true."

"Instead it was a nightmare?" Hunter guessed when she paused, lost in memories she wished she didn't have.

"Maybe just a bad dream," Terese amended, not wanting to be overly dramatic.

"What happened?"

"We got as far as the engagement party. It was a big, splashy thing that my stepmother and Eve threw us— they said someone like me getting someone like Dean to propose was an occasion bigger than man landing on the moon."

"No Terese-bashing," Hunter repeated.

"Again, just reporting the facts. The party was a huge event. Not the kind of thing I would ordinarily have wanted, but I was in such a state of…bliss, I guess you'd have to say, that I went along with anything. The whole world and everything in it just looked rosy to me."

Terese stalled, recalling that feeling, hating the crash that had come so soon after it.

"And then?" Hunter said to encourage her.

"The party had been going on for hours and I realized that I hadn't seen Dean for a while so I went looking for him."

"Don't tell me you found him with someone else?"

"Actually," Terese admitted somewhat shame-facedly, "I found him with someone else, but not in a compromising position, if that's what you're thinking. Our butler, Pixley, told me he'd seen Dean go into the library, and so I went up there looking for him. But the door was open a little and rather than going in, I stood outside and eavesdropped."

"On Dean-Dean."

"On Dean talking to his brother. Kind of arguing with his brother, actually."

"About you?"

"About Dean marrying me."

"His brother didn't approve?"

"His brother knew him," Terese said, unable to keep the sadness out of her voice. "His brother knew that Dean was involved with someone else. While I listened, Dean admitted that he was. He told his brother that there were no plans to end his relationship with the woman—whoever she was, I never knew. But he was marrying me because he was terribly in debt from school loans and apparently so was the woman he was in love with. So they'd decided it was better for him to 'hook himself a big fish.' The plan was for him to cash in as much as he could, and then get out of the marriage and have the pretty girl he really loved."

From the corner of her eye Terese saw Hunter shaking his head. "I'm sorry I asked," he said, his voice low and colored with what sounded like anger. "I hope you broke into that room and called off the engagement on the spot and then had somebody throw the guy out on his…ear."

"With a house full of guests and writers for the society pages? No, I didn't. I had to try to keep a good face on it until the end of the party—definitely not the easiest thing I've ever done. And then I told him what I'd heard."

"Did he deny it?"

"Initially. But he knew he'd been caught so it wasn't long before he accepted that I wasn't going through with marrying someone who was more attracted to my financial assets than to me."

"And *then* did you have somebody throw him out on his ear?" Hunter asked as if he would have found some satisfaction in hearing that.

It made Terese smile and somehow feel better about having trusted him with this. "No, he walked out under his own steam. And then I had to tell my family…"

"Why do I get the impression that was every bit as tough on you?"

"Eve and my stepmother thought I should have gone through with the wedding, anyway. My step-mother wasn't surprised that money had been my greatest appeal to Dean; she said it was the only rea-son any man would want to marry me. Eve agreed and advised that I just accept that I was going to have to buy myself a husband if I ever expected to have one."

They'd reached the ranch then and as Hunter pulled the truck to a stop near the barn behind the cabin he didn't say anything. But when Terese glanced over at him she saw that his jaw was clenched tight.

Only after the engine was off did he turn to her. "The Dean guy was a money-grubbing jerk and somebody should have knocked his block off. But I don't think I like your stepmother or your sister too much better."

"They aren't what you'd call supportive," she agreed with a mirthless chuckle.

"And that's why you aren't keen on the idea of marriage—you're afraid anyone who would marry you would be marrying you for your money. Or at least that you couldn't be sure one way or another," he summarized.

"I honestly never had even a thought before the engagement party that that might be a factor with Dean," Terese admitted quietly. "I guess I was just naive. But now... Now I've had my eyes opened and I know it's too big an issue *not* to have an influence."

Hunter shook his head, but Terese wasn't sure if it was in denial of that opinion or out of sympathy for her.

"I'm so sorry, Terese."

That made her smile slightly again. "You didn't do any of it."

"I know. I'm sorry anyone did. That anyone would do anything like that to you. And that your own family... You deserve so much better," he said, reaching a hand to cup the side of her face.

It was strange, but merely the touch of his hand seemed to ease most of the bad feelings brought on by talking about Dean. It made everything that had happened with Dean seem less important. As she looked into Hunter's handsome face she had the fleeting thought that Dean had only been a shallow reflection of a man, but that here was Hunter and he was the real thing...

Something about that sent a shiver through her. Hunter saw it, or felt it, and interpreted it to mean that she was cold now that the car was turned off and so was the heat.

He took his hand away and said, "Let's get you inside where it's warm." Then he got out of the truck and rounded the rear to her side to open her door.

Neither of them said anything as she got out and they headed for the cabin. The silence and the cool, clean air helped clear Terese's head of thoughts of her past, and by the time they reached her doorstep, Hunter was all she was thinking about. And the fact that even though they'd been together most of the afternoon and evening, it didn't seem as if she'd seen enough of him. Certainly not enough to send him off for two weeks.

Maybe his trip was on his mind then, too, because as she unlocked the cabin door he said, "Do you think we covered everything you need to know while I'm gone?"

"Let's see. You walked me through it all three times today. You left me lists and instructions and telephone numbers. Willy and Carla will be here every day to help and in case anything comes up that I'm not sure about…yes, I think I'm covered, don't you?"

"I s'pose I do," he said, settling a shoulder against the doorjamb as he always did when they were about to say good-night.

Terese was in her position, too, just inside and facing him. And not wanting to say good-night at all.

But Hunter didn't seem any more eager than she was because that wasn't what he did. Instead he repeated something else she already knew. "I'm leavin' here a little after 5:00 a.m."

"Mmm-hmm."

"There's no sense in you getting up that early so I guess I won't see you again before I go."

"I *could* get up." And then she could see him again and this, right now, wouldn't have to be goodbye for a whole two weeks.

"I think that would just make it tougher for me to go," Hunter said in a low voice.

"It would?" Terese asked before she'd thought about it, surprised that she might have that effect on him.

Those topaz eyes of his penetrated hers. "I've never wanted to go and leave Johnny, but all of a sudden— today especially—I keep thinkin' that I don't want to go and leave you, either."

"Because you don't trust me with Johnny?" she asked, wary of believing Hunter was saying what she thought he might be saying.

"No, I trust you with Johnny. It just struck me that he's not the only one I'm going to miss."

A second shiver took her and again he saw it. Or sensed it.

"You're really chilled tonight," he said, pushing away from the jamb and stepping inside to reach both hands to her arms. He rubbed them up and down to generate heat as she tried to think of what to say to him.

"You do have to go, though," she reminded him with an echo of regret in her own voice.

"Yeah, I do. But this last week…" He inclined his head and shrugged one of those substantial shoulders.

"I don't know. It just feels like I'm leavin' more behind than I was before."

Terese didn't know how to answer that, either, and could only look up into his sculpted face and bask in the warmth of his gaze.

As she did, time seemed to stand still. The rest of the world receded and all that remained was Hunter. And her. And being there with him like that—alone, close enough together that she could smell the scent of his aftershave and see the shadow of his beard and the lines that sunshine and laughter had begun to etch at the corners of his eyes.

And in that moment when nothing existed but the two of them, there were some things she couldn't help thinking about. Things like the fact that he was leaving in a matter of hours, and how much she wanted those hours to be special, memorable. Things like that thought she'd had earlier about how she might have passed up her only chance the night before. Things like how much more she'd regretted that as today had gone by...

As if she'd spoken what was on her mind and given him the go-ahead, Hunter tightened his grip on her arms and took yet another step closer, pulling her toward him to kiss her.

He kissed her without any hesitancy. Without any timidity. Almost as if he were picking up where they'd left off the previous evening because he knew she'd been sorry she'd ended it prematurely.

His mouth came over hers, claiming it as if he had the right. Terese met and matched him, claiming some rights of her own, even as she asked herself if she really did want to give in and just let nature take its course.

But the answer was right there, at the forefront of her brain. Nature was stronger than she was. And yes, she did want to give in to it. She wanted to stop fighting what she felt for this man. She wanted to stop fighting all he brought to the surface in her. And tonight that was exactly what she was going to do— she was going to stop fighting it.

Hunter had come far enough inside to clear the threshold, and almost by reflex Terese reached around him and pushed the door closed.

The sound ended their kiss as Hunter looked up, his eyebrows raised in question.

Now that she'd gone this far, Terese wasn't sure what to do. Or say.

But then Hunter smiled a smile tinged with wickedness and said, "Does that mean you're still cold or is it an invitation?"

"I'm not cold," she said.

"Or scared tonight?"

The way she had been the previous evening when she'd abruptly ended what had been happening between them because of her own self-doubts.

"Maybe just a little nervous," she confessed.

"But not enough to send me packin'?"

It was her turn to smile just because he was so sexy whenever he dropped his G's. "I thought you were finished packing," she challenged.

He studied her face, searched her eyes, as if to be

sure she knew what she was doing. But apparently he still wasn't convinced, because he said, "I don't want us havin' crossed signals, so I'm asking. Are you giving me the chance to stay tonight?"

Terese nodded but only barely. "If you want to," she said almost imperceptibly.

Hunter laughed. "If I want to? I didn't want to let you out of my kitchen last night. Yes, I want to."

His enthusiasm made her laugh, too. "Okay, then."

He continued to look into her eyes, to study her face, but now it was as if he couldn't get enough of the sight of her, as if he were memorizing her features. And all with a gaze so intense she could almost feel it.

He raised a hand to the side of her neck then, brushing it with the backs of his fingers as that hand rose into her hair, cupping her head to pull her even closer so he could kiss her again. Not her lips this time, though. This time he kissed her cheek, a bare meeting of supple mouth and warm breath against her skin. He kissed above her eyebrow, one then the other. He kissed her nose. And only then did his lips take hers once more. Playfully. Gently. Short, chaste kisses so intriguing that each one heightened her anticipation of the next.

And then he began to lengthen them. To linger. To draw her lips between his, separately, first the bottom, then the top, easing them apart and then returning with his parted, too. Far enough to send his tongue to lure hers.

That was when mouths opened wider and their kisses deepened.

His hands reached to her shoulders and he slipped off her coat, letting it fall to the floor behind her.

It seemed like a fine idea, so Terese did the same, discarding the jean jacket he had on and tossing it aside.

But once they'd begun, they just went on kissing and undressing each other until Terese was down to her bra and panties, and Hunter had on only his jeans, unfastened and ready to shed.

"Lights," Terese whispered between kisses that had grown hungry and seeking.

"You want it dark?" he asked.

"Please," she answered as some of her self-consciousness asserted itself.

Hunter conceded, leaving her to go to the switch near the door. But before he flipped it off, he turned to get one look at her.

It helped that his smile was full of pleasure and appreciation in response to that. It also helped that Terese got to feast on the sight of him, on the sight of those massive shoulders, those carved pectorals, those big biceps, that flat stomach and the line of dark hair that dipped from his navel to disappear into the open front of his jeans.

But still she wasn't brave enough to leave the lights on and so she said, "Off," and Hunter finally did her bidding.

He returned to her, taking one hand in his, raising

it to his lips to kiss the back of it. Then he kept hold
of it to take her across the room to the bed.

The glow of the moon coming in through the open
curtains was the only light in the cabin, just enough to
dust them in gold. Hunter kissed her again at the bedside, taking his time, holding both of her hands in his
now.

But despite the slow pace of those kisses, Terese
was feeling anything but leisurely. She wanted to know
every inch of his body, she wanted him to know every
inch of hers, she wanted all he had to offer and she
wanted it right then.

With that sense of urgency nudging her and her
hands on either side of his waist, she moved them
downward, finessing his jeans past his lean hips and
all the way off.

She felt him smile as he went on kissing her and
then he unhooked her bra and cast it aside before slipping off her panties, too.

Once they were both naked and unfettered, Hunter
wrapped his arms around her and held her close, flat-
tening her breasts to his chest where the taut knots of
her nipples greeted him impudently and letting her
feel his own need of her.

And all the while his mouth plundered hers, his
tongue toyed and taunted, and his hands massaged her
back, arousing her even just with that.

Then he lowered them both to the mattress.

Terese was on her back while Hunter lay on his
side, his big body only half over hers so he could take
her breast in one powerful hand.

Oh, but that work-roughened hand knew just the

right pressure, just the right gentleness, just the right everything to drive her out of her mind! Kneading her engorged flesh. Pulling and releasing. Rolling the very tip of her nipple against the center of his palm before fingertips took hold to tug and tease her nearly to a frenzy. She arched her back and neck at once and tore her mouth from his.

He kissed the hollow of her throat, the dip of her collarbone, and then began a descent that brought his mouth to replace his hand at her breast. Warm, wet, wonderful. He drew her deeply into that sweet darkness, flicking his tongue against the incredibly sensitive tip, circling and tormenting.

And as if that weren't enough, his hand began its own exploration, trailing soft caresses to her stomach, to her hip, down the top of her thigh and then back up the inside until he reached between her legs.

A moan escaped her throat and she couldn't help writhing beneath his touch, beneath the softest of fingers that sought and found that moist, secret part of her body, sliding into her and out again, drawing forward in a silken stroke that took the desires that had been building and making them pulsate all through her, pounding within her as loud and strong as her own heartbeat.

She filled her hands with the glories of his masculine body, tracing the muscular expanse of his back, the honed bulge of his pectorals, the tensed mounds of his perfect derriere, the sinews of his thighs and then the long, hard staff of his own desires for her, until she had him every bit as worked up as he had her.

He came above her then, fitting himself in that juncture his hand had just left wanting, capturing her mouth with his in a wide-open play of lips and tongues as that proof of his manhood found its home inside her, filling her with the greatness that was Hunter, diving in and retreating and diving in again as far as he could go.

It felt so amazing Terese could hardly breathe. *He* felt so amazing—on top her, inside of her, moving in and out, in and out with ever-increasing speed and force.

She clung to his back as he lifted her higher and higher until it was as if they'd broken free of gravity. He took her to soar in a miraculous explosion of ecstasy. Ecstasy that held her in its grip for an unbelievable moment when sensation was all that existed. One incomprehensibly astonishing sensation that melded her to him and made them a single body together in mindless perfection.

And then it dissolved like glitter floating to the ground, slowly taking them with it until Hunter enjoyed one last wave, one last deep, deep thrust that sent shudders through him now. Shudders Terese absorbed and savored.

Then, spent, he relaxed his weight completely onto her.

For a time that was how they stayed, too exhausted to do more than catch their breath.

Then Hunter pushed his upper body away from her and braced himself on his forearms to kiss her again. A slow, soft kiss.

"Tell me you're all right," he ordered afterward.

Terese smiled. "I'm all right," she complied. Then she added smugly, "Maybe even a little better than all right."

That made him laugh. "Only a *little* better than all right?"

"Quite a bit actually."

"Me, too," he nearly growled in answer.

He rolled from atop her then, taking her with him to lie by his side. He wrapped one arm around her to keep her close and reached to cup the back of her head in his other hand.

"I'll be gone when you wake up, you know," he said then.

"Mmm," was all Terese could manage because that was the last thing she wanted to think about.

"But I'll call every day."

"Um-hmm."

"And I'll be back."

"I know," she said, keeping her eyes closed so she could just revel in the feel of his warm skin under her cheek while she still had him there.

"And then we'll see," he whispered.

And then we'll see, she thought.

Not really considering what that might mean…

Eight

Terese had honestly thought she would wake up when Hunter left her bed. She'd *wanted* to wake up to say goodbye to him.

But when the sounds of Willy working near the barn and Johnny calling to him penetrated her dreams, something told her she hadn't made it.

Still, hoping Willy and Johnny were there to pick Hunter up and that she might be able to catch him, she opened her eyes.

But the sun was shining brightly through the windows and the alarm clock said seven forty-seven. Which meant that Hunter was long gone.

Just that realization was enough to make her miss him.

But he'll be back, she told herself as she got out of bed.

It was just that in the cold light of day that reasoning didn't sustain her for long. Not when her head began to fill with other thoughts, thoughts that assaulted her like sharp rocks thrown at her bare skin.

She had reason to doubt herself, her thoughts reminded her—years and years of her sister and her stepmother pointing out that she didn't have any appeal, and an engagement to a man who had said he was settling for the plain girl with money.

She thought about the vows she'd made to herself long ago not to pin her future on any man, let alone a man who was incredible-looking and could have any woman. In this case, it was a man who had already had a woman so beautiful she'd made her living from her beauty.

Her thoughts had the strength and power to override any good memories of the night before so that by the time she was showered and dressed she was wondering what had possibly possessed her to actually sleep with Hunter.

But it was too late now, she told herself with a sinking feeling. What was done was done and couldn't be taken back. And the best she could do, she decided, was cut her losses.

It was with that in mind that she made another vow to herself as she finally got ready to move her things from the cabin into the guest room in the main house to be nearer to Johnny. She vowed to go through the next two weeks putting all her energy, all her focus, into her nephew. He was the reason she was at the ranch. He was what mattered and she had precious little time remaining with him.

And while she was enjoying that time with him she swore she would do everything she possibly could not to think about his father. To try to forget that that night together had ever happened.

And she absolutely would not think about what might happen when Hunter got back.

Or get her hopes up...

It wasn't difficult for Terese to keep that vow to put all her energy and focus into Johnny during the two weeks that followed. Her nephew was a joy to Terese and she loved every minute of playing at being his mom—even the minutes when he was cranky or out-of-sorts or showing a stubborn streak.

Those times were infrequent, anyway, because, for the most part he wanted to please her as much as she wanted to please him. In fact, he didn't even put up a fuss going to their doctors' appointments on Wednesday of that first week, and instead did his best to comfort and support her through having her blood drawn for the test for hemophilia.

But still, Hunter was never too far from Terese's mind.

She didn't want to think about him. To miss him. To imagine what it would be like if he not only came home to Johnny, but came home to her, too. Sometimes even her best efforts weren't enough to stop it, especially not when he called every day.

Terese made sure that most of the time Hunter was on the telephone, he was talking to Johnny, and kept her conversations with him brief and impersonal.

Still, whenever he took up residence in her thoughts, whenever she'd had even a moment to touch base with him, she was vigilant about reminding herself that there hadn't been any discussion about what would happen when he did come back. There hadn't been any hint that things would be any different just because they'd made love. And the only thing Hunter had said was *And then we'll see*—which certainly wasn't any kind of promise.

Hunter was scheduled to return on Saturday—two weeks to the day after he'd left. On the day before that, Terese had another doctor's appointment to learn the results of her blood test. So, after taking Johnny to his favorite hamburger restaurant for lunch, the two of them went to Portland General Hospital again.

"You're sure I don't have to do anything?" Johnny asked as they went in the hospital's front doors.

"I'm sure," Terese told the little boy. "This visit is only for me and it's just a talking visit, anyway. It's called a consultation."

"They aren't gonna poke you with any needles this time, either?"

"No, no needles," she assured.

"'Cuz I'd hold your hand again if you wanted me to."

Terese rubbed her nephew's head. "I know you would and I'm grateful for that. You can still come in with me, though," she added, "and play with your drawing board while I talk to the doctor."

They reached the office then and Terese signed in before she guided Johnny to the waiting area. There were only two other people standing just beyond the small space in the corridor and Terese recognized them both. They were the same couple she'd seen at the restaurant the night she and Hunter had gone to the Parents Adoption Network meeting and then had dinner.

The woman was once again dressed in a nurse's uniform, only now she carried a stack of file folders, and Terese recalled that Hunter had said her name was Nancy. She remembered the man's name from seeing it on his ID badge that night—the same ID badge he was wearing now. He was Everett Baker from Accounting.

Once again Terese found herself in the awkward position of being unable to avoid eavesdropping on their conversation because it was impossible not to overhear what they were saying in the quiet, nearly deserted waiting area.

"I just don't understand," the nurse was saying. "I thought things between us were going well, but now you're keeping your distance."

"I've just been… Well, you know how it is… There's been a lot of work and… Well, work and well, things…" the man said, sounding shy, fumbling for his words—not at all the way he'd been at the restaurant.

"I've seen you in the cafeteria a couple of times just

staring off into space. Is everything all right with you?" the nurse persisted.

"Fine. Fine. Everything is fine."

"Because I'm a good listener. I mean, if you should ever want to talk…"

Even though Terese was trying not to look directly at the couple, she still had the impression that the man was tempted to open up to the woman. He even started a few sentences before cutting himself off, as if he were squelching the impulse to say more.

Then he finally said, "No, no, there's nothing I need to talk about. But I have missed your company," he added. "And if I've hurt your feelings, I'm sorry."

"It's not so much that. I just hope you're okay."

"Fine, I'm fine," he repeated. "In fact I'm so fine that maybe we could have dinner again this weekend—if you're not busy."

That brightened the nurse's spirits considerably. "I'm not busy, no," she said eagerly. "How about tomorrow night?"

The man agreed to dinner Saturday night but still Terese had the sense that something else was going on with him, because his enthusiasm seemed to wane suddenly, as if he wasn't certain he'd done the right thing. It was actually an odd dance to watch because the man kept drawing near and then backing away— verbally and physically—as if he was tempted to get close to the woman but fearful of it, too.

In the end he appeared to be too drawn to the nurse

to resist, and they made their plans while Terese continued to pretend she wasn't listening.

"Tomorrow night. Seven o'clock," the nurse confirmed.

Then the man told her he had to make a phone call, and when he turned to go, the nurse noticed Johnny and asked what he was building with the connecting blocks he was so interested in.

Terese was just relieved not to be in the position of eavesdropping any longer and listened to her nephew explain that he was making a barn like the one his dad kept their horses in.

Everett Baker could see the waiting room from the small alcove he'd ducked into not far away and for a moment before he went in he stopped to watch Nancy chatting with the little boy.

Had he done the right thing by making plans to see her again? he kept asking himself.

He *had* been trying to keep his distance from her because he was so worried about blowing his cover. But there was just a part of him that couldn't resist her sweet appeal.

Maybe it would be all right, he told himself. Maybe he could keep things separate. And she was a good source of information that he could use to his benefit.

A twinge of guilt for using Nancy like that niggled at him but he ignored it. *All's fair in love and war,* he thought. And this was a little of both.

Nancy finished talking to the child and went on

her way, so Everett stepped deeper into the alcove for privacy.

The call he had to make couldn't be made on his work phone so once he was certain no one was anywhere around, he pulled his cell phone from his jacket pocket.

"Just a quick check," he muttered to himself when he pushed the button to speed-dial his party.

When the other end of the line was picked up, Everett spun around to face the wall and in a hushed voice without identifying himself, he said, "Did you make the delivery?"

Confirmation came with the same cold, ruthless tone he was using and since that was all Everett needed to know, he ended the call as abruptly as he'd made it.

He turned off his phone and replaced it in his jacket pocket, unable to keep the smug smile from curling his lips.

So the hand-off of the stolen ovarian eggs—ripe for in-vitro fertilization—was complete, he thought. Good.

And he was going to get to see Nancy again tomorrow night. That was good, too.

All in all, a good day for Everett Baker.

And no one deserved it more.

At least as far as he was concerned.

"Ms. Warwick? You can come in now, the doctor is ready to see you."

"T'rese says I can come, too. 'Cuz it's just a consolation and nobody's doin' nothin' with needles."

Terese laid a hand to the top of Johnny's head and told the nurse, "He's with me."

The nurse nodded and led them to the doctor's office where the hematologist was sitting behind his desk, looking over papers.

When Terese and Johnny were shown in, he glanced up, greeted them and asked them to take a seat.

There were two chairs in front of his desk. Terese sat in one and nodded toward the couch that was against the wall to the side of them. "You can sit there and draw if you want, Johnny."

"No, that's okay," the little boy answered, climbing onto the second chair as if he needed to lend her moral support.

The doctor exchanged amenities with them both and then got down to business.

"I was just looking over the results of your blood test," he began. "I'm happy to tell you that you are not a carrier of hemophilia."

That was a relief to Terese and she told him so.

Then the doctor surprised her and said, "There's more."

"Oh?"

"Don't be alarmed, you're fine. Very healthy, in fact. It's just that when I order the blood work I have the lab run the whole gamut of tests so we get a complete picture of what we're dealing with should the patient prove to carry the hemophilia gene. That includes a pregnancy test."

"A pregnancy test?" Terese repeated a bit dimly, trying to assimilate the turn this conversation had taken. "Yes. And I hope this is news you want to hear—the test was positive."

"Positive? How can that be? I mean, my—" She suddenly became very aware of Johnny and said, "I'm not even late yet. I'm just due in the next day or two."

"The blood test is far more accurate than urine tests. It can detect the hormones within days of conception. And although the levels are low, telling us you're in the very early stages, you are most definitely pregnant."

Terese's head went light and her mouth went dry and she still couldn't believe what she was hearing. "You're kidding," she said.

The gray-haired man across the desk shook his head. "No, I'm not kidding."

"There couldn't be some kind of mistake? Or mix-up or wrong reading or something?"

"We're very careful," the doctor assured, looking less convinced that he was delivering good news. But that still didn't change what he was saying. "I just hope congratulations are in order because there's no doubt about it. You are going to have a baby."

Terese drove back to the ranch half-dazed.

Pregnant, she kept thinking over and over again. *I'm pregnant.*

She'd honestly believed that that would never be a part of life she would experience. After Dean and the pain she'd suffered, it was as if she'd put her hopes and dreams of having a family on a very, very high shelf. Out of reach.

Not because he had finally convinced her that she wasn't attractive enough for any man to want. But because Dean had disillusioned her to such an extent, hurt her so much, that she'd made a conscious, firm decision never to open herself up to the possibility of that happening again. She would never allow herself to suspect the possibility that a man would be settling for her. She'd made a decision never to allow herself to be that vulnerable again. Never to let another man get so close that she planned a future with him only to learn it wasn't her that he wanted.

And with that decision came the realization that she wouldn't have kids.

It was something she'd come to accept. Not to like, but to accept.

Only now here she was, pregnant.

Now she *would* have a child. A child of her own.

Hunter's child.

"T'rese? We're home. Are we gonna get out of the car?"

Terese had been so distracted that she'd gotten them back to the ranch, parked her car and turned off the engine, all with only just enough awareness to do it safely. She didn't know how long she'd been sitting there before Johnny's question reminded her of their arrival.

She jolted out of her thoughts then and tried to pretend everything was normal.

"Out of the car and into the house. It looks like Willie and Carla are already here. Carla was bringing dinner over tonight," she said too cheerfully.

"Carla said she'd make her pumpkin cake, too! I hope she did."

"Why don't you go in and see if she did? I'm just going to sit here for a minute yet," Terese said.

Johnny didn't hesitate to take her suggestion. He unfastened his seatbelt and bounded out of the car, running to the house and disappearing inside while Terese watched him go.

She knew she was expected to follow him. To go into that house with Johnny and Carla and Willy, to spend the evening with them all, to go with them tomorrow to the airport to pick up Hunter when his plane came in. And she would need to do it all as if nothing had changed.

Only for her, everything had.

She was pregnant with Hunter's baby!

Hunter—who would be home tomorrow.

The full impact of that fact began to penetrate.

How was she supposed to handle that? Was she supposed to meet him at the airport and announce he was going to be a father for the second time? He'd think she was crazy.

And what else would he think?

That question popped into her mind on its own, but once it had, she couldn't ignore it.

What else *would* Hunter think? And equally as important, how would he react? What would he do?

The cockeyed optimist in her wanted to think he would whisk her into his arms and be thrilled.

But the realist in her just couldn't buy into that.

The realist in her pointed out that there weren't any ties between them. That spending one night together didn't constitute a commitment. That the most Hunter had said after that one night was, *And then we'll see....*

The realist in her pointed out that he hadn't been widowed for long, that he hadn't even dated since he'd lost his wife, and that he'd said he'd put a moratorium on getting involved with anyone so he could keep Johnny his central focus.

Given all that, was he likely to be thrilled that she was pregnant? To whisk her into his arms and make all her dreams come true?

Terese didn't think so. Or at least she didn't think he was likely to do it willingly. Or gladly.

But was he likely to feel trapped? Maybe even obligated to marry her?

She knew Hunter well enough to know that he wouldn't shirk any responsibility. Certainly not one to a child of his own making. So yes, she thought he would feel obligated to marry her. And under those circumstances, how could he feel anything *but* trapped?

Marrying her out of obligation was not the same as marrying her because he was in love with her. It wasn't the same as marrying her because he couldn't live without her. It wasn't the same as marrying her because he felt about her the way he'd felt about his late wife.

But it *was* very nearly the same as Dean planning to marry her for her money.

That thought stopped her cold.

If Hunter were to marry her, it would only be because he *had* to.

In a way, this was even worse than what Dean had been about to do because this wouldn't even be something Hunter had chosen to do willingly.

So what was she going to do? she asked herself.

She could tell Hunter about the baby, make it clear that she wasn't interested in marriage, that she didn't need his financial help, that she didn't expect anything from him.

But what if he ignored all that and tried to persuade her that they should get married, anyway?

It would be so tempting.

She didn't want to put a name to her feelings for Hunter, but the feelings were strong all the same. And Hunter had Johnny. It would be so nice to be included in their little family, to add to it.

But if she gave in to that temptation, she knew she would always be left with the knowledge that Hunter wasn't with her for any of the reasons she wanted him to be with her. She would know what she would have known if she'd gone through with marrying Dean—that Hunter didn't really want *her.* She would know that their marriage was just the shallow, superficial, empty shell of a marriage she'd promised herself she'd never have.

"So that only leaves one option," she said out loud in the stillness of the car.

Not to let Hunter know about the baby at all. To consider this *her* baby and her baby alone. Then Hunter wouldn't feel trapped or obligated or responsible. He just wouldn't know. And for him, ignorance could be bliss.

Certainly it would be better than to be bound to a marriage he didn't want, to a person he didn't want. A person who could never live up to his first wife.

It wasn't the perfect solution. It wasn't even a solution Terese was proud of. But right then, still half in shock over what she'd learned only an hour before, it seemed like the best thing to do for everyone involved. She would have the baby she'd never thought she'd be able to have and be thankful for the rest of her life for that gift Hunter had given her. And Hunter would be free to find another wife—when he was ready to— who could make him feel all his first wife had made him feel.

"But there's still tonight and tomorrow to get through," she reminded herself.

And she didn't know how she could possibly get through the time pretending that she hadn't just heard the biggest news of her life.

She didn't know how she could face Hunter, how she could look into those wonderful eyes of his, how she could feast on the sight of that handsome face, and act as if something monumental hadn't happened between them.

So there was only one thing she could think to do.

She would go inside, tell Carla and Willy that

something had come up at home and she needed to leave immediately.

They would stay and take care of Johnny—she knew that was no problem—and they'd pick up Hunter at the airport tomorrow, too.

And then all of their lives would go on just the way they had before she and Hunter had ever met.

But the idea of leaving Johnny even a little earlier than she'd thought she'd have to wrenched Terese's heart suddenly. That she might not see him again hurt even worse.

Too much worse to accept.

She had to see Johnny again. That was all there was to it.

If she could arrange to see him alone, Hunter still wouldn't have to know she was pregnant. And if he *did* find out down the road, then she could say the baby belonged to someone else.

Again, it wasn't a perfect solution. But hoping it might work was all Terese had to hang on to because she couldn't imagine leaving here in the next hour or so and never seeing her nephew again.

She decided she would just do whatever she had to do to make it work.

She took a deep breath, held it a minute and blew it out very, very slowly.

A baby. She was going to have a baby. A baby of her own.

Anything she had to do because of that was worth it, she told herself.

Even saying goodbye to Johnny earlier than she'd planned to and having to plot how to see him again later.

Even not seeing Hunter again at all.

Although the sharp stab of pain that went through her when she thought that made her wonder if it was true.

Nine

Hunter's plane landed at 3:05 Saturday afternoon. When he got to baggage claim he was surprised not to find Terese waiting for him with Johnny, Willy and Carla.

"She went home," Carla told him when he asked where Terese was. "She came back from her doctor's appointment yesterday, sent Johnny in alone, and when she came in a little while later she said something had come up and she had to leave. She asked if we'd stay the night with Johnny and pick you up today without her. Then she packed her things, said a long goodbye to Johnny and left before we even had dinner."

"Maybe something happened at home," Hunter said, as if it was no big deal to him that she wasn't with them.

But it was a big deal to him, and it was on his mind the whole way back to the ranch—even as he filled everyone in on his trip and then got the update on the homefront. It was on his mind through the dinner Carla fixed for them all, and even as he gave Johnny his bath and read him three bedtime stories.

Hunter didn't bring up Terese's name again, and he didn't ask any more questions until Johnny mentioned her himself as Hunter was tucking him in.

"I wish T'rese was still here," the boy said when he'd slid under the covers.

"I thought she would be," Hunter said. "At least for today. Did she say anything to you about why she was leaving?"

Johnny shook his head. "But she was sad. She kinda cried when she told me g'bye and she said she'd miss me horrible."

"Did she say she'd see you again?"

"I told her that I didn't want her to go, but she said she had to and that she'd try to see me again, but it might not be for kinda a while. She said she didn't want me to forget her and she'd be sendin' me stuff in the mail."

Hunter hesitated to ask the next question rattling around in his brain. He'd been so careful not to let on that things between himself and Terese had reached an emotional level. But because they had, it was all the more difficult to understand why she would take off without a word to him, a note to explain what was going on. And so he *had* to ask.

"Did she say anything about me? Or maybe give you a message to give me that you forgot about?"

Johnny did another negative shake of his head where it rested on his pillow. "Nope."

Something else had occurred to Hunter, and even though he thought it was farfetched that his son could know the answer, he allowed himself one more question. "Do you know what the doctor told her yesterday? Did she get bad news?"

"She got news. That's what the doctor said—he had news for her."

"Did you go in to see the doctor with her?"

"Uh-huh. It was only a consolation so she said I could go in with her and that was when the doctor said he had the news for her," the sleepy little boy said.

It took Hunter a moment to understand that *consolation* meant *consultation* and that that was the reason Terese had taken Johnny in with her.

Hunter didn't feel good about invading Terese's privacy but he couldn't help wondering if she'd learned she carried the hemophilia gene and if maybe that explained her abrupt departure. So he said, "Do you remember what the doctor told her?"

"Uh-huh, I heard it. She doesn't got what I got— the hemolilia—and she's gonna have a baby."

Hunter wasn't sure he'd heard that correctly. "She doesn't carry the hemophilia gene and what?"

"She's gonna have a baby," Johnny repeated, clearly without any idea of the importance of that information.

"A baby?" Hunter echoed.

"She was surprised, too, but the doctor said the blood test could tell it early or somethin' and he said congratulations. Then T'rese looked kinda funny and she didn't say much all the way home and then she left."

Johnny's eyelids closed as if they were just too heavy for him to keep open and he rolled over onto his side, completely unaware of the thunderbolt he'd just delivered to his father.

"I gotta go to sleep now," he said, his words slurring as he drifted off.

"Okay. Sleep tight," Hunter muttered, bending over to kiss his son good-night.

Then he slipped out of the room, feeling as if he'd been blindsided.

Terese was *pregnant?*

Could Johnny possibly be right? Or had he misheard or misunderstood? Maybe the doctor had said something about Terese not having to worry about having a baby because she hadn't tested positive for the hemophilia gene.

Except that Johnny had said that the doctor had told Terese that the blood test could tell she was pregnant early. And that the doctor had said congratulations...

Hunter had reached the living room by then and he half fell, half sat in the middle of the sofa, staring into space, thinking again, *Terese is pregnant?*

Could it have happened that night before he'd left? Could the blood test have detected it *this* early?

Maybe she was involved with someone else, some-one from before they'd ever met.

But even as he considered that, he didn't believe it. He knew she'd been hurt and that hurt had caused her to swear off relationships. He also knew Terese wasn't the kind of woman who slept around. No, if she was pregnant, the baby had to be his.

But how could that be?

Okay, so they hadn't used protection. And a single night without protection was enough, he admitted.

And if the doctor had said the blood test could tell early…

She really could be pregnant with his baby.

No matter how many times he repeated it to him-self in his head, it still didn't ring true.

Of all the things Hunter had thought about on his trip and the whole plane ride home, this had not been one of them. And he'd thought about Terese a lot. Al-most constantly, in fact, with only Johnny running neck-and-neck with her.

He'd thought about how good Terese was with Johnny, how patient she was with him, how much she loved him and doted on him, how kind and sweet she was, and how touching it was to see her with him.

He'd thought about how much he'd enjoyed every minute he'd spent with her himself. Every minute since she'd arrived at the ranch. He'd thought about how she made his blood run faster just by walking into a room.

He'd thought about how pretty she was—whether she believed it or not.

He'd thought about how easy she was to talk to.

How well she'd fit into their little family. How she'd stirred things inside him that had been dormant for a long time.

He'd sure as hell thought about that last night together and how incredible it had been.

But he'd never thought she might have ended up pregnant from that last night.

Pregnant.

Oh, man...

Hunter jammed his hands through his hair. Then he grasped the top of the cushions behind him and dropped his head back, too, to stare up at the ceiling.

Pregnant...

He'd also thought a lot about what would happen when he got back here. About Terese inevitably leaving. About how rotten it made him feel to think of not seeing her as much as he had. Or maybe not at all. But unlike the rest of his thoughts about her, he hadn't liked that one. He'd shied away from it each time it had popped into his head. And he hadn't come up with any idea about how to continue what had begun between them.

Now here he was, and she was gone, and all of a sudden everything was a whole lot more complicated than just trying to figure out if he was going to ask her to a movie and dinner, or to do something with him and Johnny, or to visit for a weekend here and there.

Pregnant...

Terese was going to have a baby...

His baby...

So if she was pregnant with his child, where was she? he thought, getting a little angry suddenly. Why wasn't she here telling him that they were going to have a baby? Why had she taken off before he got home, without giving him so much as a clue about what was going on and what she wanted to happen now?

If he was going to be a father again, he had the right to know that. To know where they stood. What the hell was she thinking just to take off? What was she feeling?

That last thought stayed with him, cooling him off as quickly as his temper had flared.

What *was* she feeling? he couldn't help wondering.

She had to have been as shocked as he was.

But was she happy about it?

He couldn't imagine that she wouldn't be. At least when the surprise wore off. He'd seen for himself how crazy she was about Johnny. He knew she'd thought she would never have kids of her own and had regretted that.

So once she got used to the idea, he thought she'd probably be glad.

But what about him? How did he feel about it? he asked himself.

A baby. He was going to have a baby. A brother or sister for Johnny…

He'd always wanted more than one child. He and Margee had planned to adopt at least a second baby and maybe a third. But when Margee had died, he'd had to accept that Johnny would be the only child he ever had. And now that it seemed as though that wasn't true, he tried the possibility on like a new pair of boots. Judging how it fit.

He didn't hate the idea, he realized.

In fact, the longer he considered it, the more he liked it.

He and Terese were going to have a baby….

But fast on the heels of that thought, it occurred to him that there really wasn't a "he and Terese." And that set him back a little.

It wasn't as if they were a couple, he reminded himself. It wasn't as if they'd talked about a future together or made a commitment. They were just two people, connected by Johnny, brought together over Johnny, with no other ties. Except the baby they would have now.

For the life of him, Hunter didn't know where they were supposed to go from here. He didn't even know where he *wanted* them to go from here.

The ceiling didn't hold any answers for him and he sat up straight again, staring at nothing in particular while he tried to sort out his feelings.

Where did he want them to go from here?

He knew that he'd wanted to come home to Terese as much as he'd wanted to come home to Johnny. That he'd missed her every bit as much.

He knew that coming back and finding her gone had left a hole in him, an empty spot that needed her to fill it.

He knew that the house seemed too quiet, too still, without her. That even just knowing she wasn't anywhere on the ranch made the whole place seem a little lonely.

He knew that the thought of getting up tomorrow morning and not having her across the breakfast table from him made him feel bad. Really bad. That the thought of *never* having her across the breakfast table from him made him feel even worse.

And that let him know for sure that he wanted her here.

But the more he thought about it, the more he realized he didn't just want her here in the general proximity the way she'd been before. He wanted her here in his house. In his bed. In his life. Here helping him raise Johnny and having their new baby.

Only *here* was a long way from where Terese had come from, he reminded himself. *Here* was a modest but rustic ranch, while she was accustomed to a mansion, an entire estate complete with servants and drivers and gardeners and more amenities than he would ever be able to give her.

So maybe she wouldn't want to be here.

Somehow he didn't believe that any more than he believed she might have slept with another man.

Terese hadn't seemed to care that staying at the ranch was such a step down from the way she usually lived. At least she hadn't seemed to care over the short term. Would she feel differently over the long term?

He didn't think so. Not when he recalled their picnic dinner when she'd eaten the marshmallow Johnny had dropped in the dirt. Not when he pictured her happily cooking in his simple kitchen. Not when he recalled how willing she was to pitch in, to lend a hand with Johnny or Johnny's chores. Not when he thought of how much she seemed to enjoy the simple stay-at-home socializing they'd done with Carla and Willy.

There was just something down-to-earth about Terese, something the exact opposite of her pretentious sister. Something that let him think—or at least hope—that she might not care too much about leaving behind the perks of her wealth and social standing if he asked her to.

But what about his own vows not to let himself be taken away from Johnny by a relationship with a woman? *Taken away from Johnny*—that was what Hunter had envisioned happening if he let a woman into their lives. He'd seen himself torn between the woman and his son. He'd seen the attention he might pay a woman costing Johnny the attention that was his due. He'd seen being involved with a woman as cheating his son by dividing his time, his energy.

But that wasn't how it had been with Terese. As much as she'd drawn his attention, his thoughts, it hadn't been as if anything was being taken away from Johnny. He'd still done the same things he'd always done with his son; Terese had just been included, too.

And rather than Johnny losing anything, he'd actually gained. He'd gained Terese's attention, Terese's love and affection, Terese's delight in him.

No, nothing about her had subtracted from his son. When it came to Terese, the truth was that she had only added to Johnny's life. Which was probably why Johnny liked her as much as he did.

And Johnny *did* like her. Hadn't he wanted to "keep" her?

Keep her...

"That's just what I want to do," Hunter said out loud when the reality finally gelled for him.

He wanted to keep Terese.

And he wanted to keep her for good.

For himself.

For his son.

New baby or no new baby.

Hunter pushed himself off the couch then and made a beeline for the telephone.

He couldn't very well wake up his son and drag him with him, so he needed someone to come to the ranch and stay with the sleeping Johnny while he did what he suddenly couldn't wait to do. He called Willy and arranged for him and Carla to come back.

Then he went up the stairs two at a time and charged into his bathroom to shower and change out of the clothes he'd traveled home in.

Wondering the whole way if there was any chance he could get Terese back here before this night was through.

Ten

"Finally! I thought you were going to make us late for our table again."

When Eve Warwick opened the front door to the Warwick mansion it was clear that Hunter was not who she thought to find standing on the doorstep. He wasn't thrilled to see her, either, but he had more manners than to let it show the way Eve did.

Her overly made-up face dissolved into a sneer and she said, "You again."

"I'm afraid so," Hunter confirmed.

"You're making me very sorry I ever allowed an open adoption."

"Relax. I'm not here to see you," he informed her unceremoniously.

He'd thought about Eve as he'd driven to the War-wick estate, about the fact that if this visit accom-plished what he wanted it to accomplish, he—and Johnny—would end up with Johnny's birth mother in their life. It wasn't a scenario that sat well with him.

But he'd come to the conclusion that the positives of having Terese in their lives outweighed the nega-tives of having Eve.

Besides, he'd believed Terese when she'd said she seldom saw her sister even though they shared the same house, that Eve traveled and only made pit stops in Portland. He had hopes that if Terese lived with him and Johnny at the ranch they could have the same kind of relationship with Eve that he had with his brother—basically a nonexistent one that involved rarely, if ever, seeing each other. And since he felt sure that was the way Eve would want it, too, he'd decided to forge ahead in spite of her.

"I'm here to see Terese," Hunter said then, stepping into the foyer without an invitation and thereby forc-ing Eve to give way.

"Surely the blood bank has replenished its supply of AB negative by now and you don't need a direct donor," the haughty woman responded.

"This isn't about her blood. It's personal."

That made Eve laugh. An ugly laugh. "Personal," she repeated facetiously. "As in what? Something *ro-mantic?* Now wouldn't that be too droll? Don't tell me that Plain Jane has roped herself a hunky cowboy? Just between you and me, you could do a lot better."

"Is that so? And that would be according to you—the expert on things like that?"

Eve missed his sarcasm. "Your wife, for instance," she said. "Your wife was better. She was a model, wasn't she? And very beautiful, if I'm remembering correctly. After that, surely you don't expect me to believe you're attracted to Terese."

Hunter tried to hold on to his temper but it wasn't easy. "There was a lot more to my late wife than just the way she looked. In the same way, there's a lot more to Terese. She has qualities some other people should envy," he ended pointedly.

"*Other people* being me?" Eve sneered again, catching his meaning. "I don't need the qualities Terese has. My qualities are obvious. And well appreciated."

"And all on the surface," Hunter added. "But me? I'll take someone with more substance, thank you very much. So, I'd like to talk to Terese."

"Let's see…It's Saturday night…Where would Terese be? Out on the town with men clamoring just to sit next to her and gaze into her beautiful face? No, that doesn't sound like Terese. Hmm…Oh, yes, now I remember. She's in the library. Alone as always."

"Do you want to let her know I'm here or just point me in the right direction?"

"I'm about to be picked up by my date. The library is down the hall, third door on the left. Be my guest and surprise her."

* * *

Hunter couldn't surprise Terese because she was within hearing distance of the foyer and had realized he was there when he'd come into the house.

But she hadn't left the library. Instead she'd stayed just inside the half-open door, listening to the exchange between Hunter and her sister. And wondering what to do.

Just knowing he was so near made her heart beat fast and hard and her head go light.

But she couldn't let herself get carried away. She had to keep in mind why she'd left the ranch in the first place. She had to keep in mind that she was pregnant and that she didn't want him to know it, didn't want him offering a future possibly only because of it.

It was just that some of what he'd said to her sister kept repeating itself in her mind—the fact that he thought she had a lot of qualities, substance, and that he preferred substance to surface.

It would be embarrassing to have him guess that she'd been listening, though, and when she heard his bootsteps draw nearer to the library she hurried back to the leather chair she'd been sitting in, as if she'd never left it.

A gentle tap on the door announced him and the door opened all the way and there he was.

"Can I come in?"

Terese tried to look surprised. "Hunter. Where did you come from?" she said, all the while devouring her first glimpse of him in two weeks.

Tall and lean, he was wearing boots, tight jeans, a black turtleneck sweater and a denim jacket that all worked together to make him look even better than she remembered—if that was possible.

"Your sister let me in and sent me back to find you," he said.

He stepped completely into the room then and closed door behind him, leaning against it as if to block anyone else's entrance.

For a long moment he just stayed like that, looking at her, studying her.

His scrutiny didn't help put her at ease even though she wasn't worried about how she was dressed. Her hair was pulled up into a twist at the crown of her head, and she had on a perfectly acceptable pair of gray slacks and a charcoal-colored cardigan sweater. But he didn't seem to care what she was wearing. She had the sense that his eyes were searching for more than mere appearances.

When she couldn't bear the silence any longer, she said, "Is Johnny okay?"

Hunter was slow to answer and even when he did he preceded it with a nod of his head. "Johnny's fine. Sound asleep at home with Carla and Willy before I ever left the house. He doesn't even know I'm gone."

"And is everything else all right?" Terese asked, trying not to squirm beneath the intensity in his topaz gaze.

"No, as a matter of fact, everything isn't all right," he said pointedly. "I came home today as eager to see you as I was to see Johnny and you weren't there. You were gone. Without so much as a see-you-around."

"Something came up," she said quickly—too quickly—wishing she'd thought of a good lie to go with that vague excuse. But it had been enough to get her out of the house the night before and since she hadn't expected to see Hunter again anytime soon she hadn't put thought into expanding it. Especially with so much else on her mind.

"I wondered if you'd had bad news at the doctor's office yesterday," Hunter said then. "But Johnny tells me you don't carry the hemophilia gene."

"No, it was good news," she confirmed, beginning to worry what else Johnny might have told him about her doctor's visit. And wondering why it hadn't occurred to her that her nephew might relay what he'd heard yesterday. *All* of what he'd heard.

"He said you had good news," Hunter confirmed.

And in that minute, in the tone of his voice, Terese knew Hunter knew the doctor had told her she was pregnant.

She just didn't know what to do about it.

So she remained sitting there, very still, feeling the beat of her heart again.

"Johnny's only four, you know," Hunter said. "He doesn't always get things right. So how about I tell you what he told me and you can tell me if it's true?"

Terese couldn't sit calmly in that chair another minute. She got up and went to the fireplace as if the fire needed checking, saying nothing to encourage Hunter.

"Terese?" he said to bring her attention back to him when she'd prodded the burning logs longer than necessary.

You're not going to be able to avoid this, she lectured herself. *You'll just have to see it through and stick to your guns.*

She took a deep breath, squared her shoulders and moved to the desk, trying to draw support from it by leaning on it and holding tight to the edge with both hands hidden behind her hips in a white-knuckled grip.

Only then did she look at Hunter again and when she did she could see that he'd come with a clear purpose in mind, that nothing was going to stop him.

And she was right because he said, "Johnny told me that the doctor said you're going to have a baby."

Terese closed her eyes.

Apparently the shock of hearing that from the doctor had dulled her wits because suddenly she knew her plans for everything since then had been feeble. It hadn't occurred to her that Johnny had taken in what the doctor had told her. Or that he would understand enough to repeat it. But of course he had. Of course he would report what he'd heard. And of course once Hunter had found out, Terese leaving the ranch wasn't enough to keep him away.

And without knowing what else to do, Terese said, "This time Johnny got it right."

"So you are pregnant?" Hunter said, his voice low.

"According to the doctor, the blood test can detect the elevation in hormone levels right away—within days of conception."

"And you found out and ran?" he asked in disbelief.

"I didn't think of it as *running*."

"What did you think of it as?"

Terese shrugged. "There were a lot of things going through my mind. It was the biggest shock I've ever had. But mainly I just didn't want you feeling any kind of…obligation."

"Obligation…" Hunter echoed the word as if it had no place there. Then he said, "Did it occur to you that I might feel other things?"

"Like what?" she said, making it clear through her own tone that she hadn't considered anything else.

"That I might be happy about it?"

"Happy that one impulsive night together produced an unplanned pregnancy? With me, of all people? No, that definitely didn't occur to me."

"With you of all people?"

"Yes, me of all people. It's not as if you picked me out of a crowd or met me at a party and said 'that's the woman for me.' I'm the Plain Jane whom you had to let into your life because of unfortunate circumstances and only let into your house because you felt as if you owed it to me after I gave blood for Johnny."

Hunter stared at her for another long moment before he shook his head with what looked like more disbelief. "Okay, that was how things started out. But that isn't how they ended up. *You of all people* are the only person I've gotten close enough to in the last two years to think about every waking minute of every day since I first set eyes on you. *You of all people* are the only person I've felt like myself with, the only person I've let down my guard with, the only person I've really let in at all. *You of all people* are the only person who's made me feel alive again. The only person I've wanted…"

Terese hadn't known he felt that way.

Or did he?

He said it all as if he genuinely meant it and she wanted to believe it—more than she'd ever wanted to believe anything. But now that she knew he knew she was pregnant, it was difficult.

"But you wanted a night, maybe, not a baby and a tie to me forever," she insisted.

"You thought you were just a one-night-stand?"

"I wasn't really thinking," she confessed. "I was just…feeling. Getting carried away. And so were you. That's the point."

"And then I spent two weeks without you and things fell into place for me. That's what happens, you know, when you find yourself missing someone so much you can hardly think about anything else. It's what happens when you can't sleep at night because you just want that person there with you. It's what happens when everything you see makes you think of that other person, when the food you eat, the feel of the sunshine on your face, the smell in the air makes you remember something about them. It's what happens when you count the hours until you can make a simple phone call to hear their voice, when you count the days until you can see them again. When your whole body aches for them…"

He paused to let his eyes bore into her once more and then he said, "What happens is that you come back knowing that you want more than one impulsive night of getting carried away."

"But not a baby."

Something about that made him smile a bit wryly. "Okay, so no, a baby is a whole new extreme. But that doesn't mean it's bad. It doesn't change any of what I came home thinking and feeling and wanting."

"You came home thinking about maybe seeing me again after I left the ranch, not having a baby with me. And that changes everything."

"Actually, after my four-year-old gave me the news that I was going to be a father again," Hunter began with a note of facetiousness, "I did a lot of thinking about what a baby changes. But what it doesn't change—what dating you would have proven—is that I don't want just to date you. Dating you wouldn't have brought you back to the ranch. It wouldn't have gotten you there every morning when I wake up and every night when I go to sleep. It wouldn't have gotten you there with Johnny and me every day. And that's what I really want, Terese. I really want just to have you with me, with Johnny, every day, every minute, in our house and in our lives."

Again Terese wanted to believe him. But she didn't have any experience with someone wanting her for herself, and so she said, "Because of the baby."

That made Hunter shake his head—forcefully and with a dark expression on his handsome face. "Because of you," he repeated, carefully, slowly enunciating each word.

He pushed away from the door then and came to stand directly in front of her. "I know what you're thinking," he said. "I know you're thinking that that other guy said he wanted you when all he really wanted was your money. I know now you're thinking that I'm here saying I want you only because you're pregnant. But you're wrong. Johnny and I wanted to keep you even before this."

"*Keep* me?"

"It was Johnny's phrase. When I was packing for the trip he asked me what was going to happen with you when I got back and he said he wanted to keep you. And the longer I thought about it, the more I realized that I do, too. And the reason I do is I'm in love with you, Terese. Pregnant or not pregnant."

He was standing so near that she could smell his aftershave, she could see the creases at the corners of his eyes, she could almost feel the heat of him. But more than what was right there in front of her, she began to think about what she knew of the man himself.

Hunter Coltrane wasn't the same kind of man Dean Wittiker had been. And not only in the fact that he worked for what he had, that the one time she'd been afraid he might be after money from her he'd proved her wrong. Hunter was a man without any pretenses. He was an honest man, a plain and simple man of strong character and solid values. And while he was also a man who would feel compelled to do the right thing by her and his baby, he wouldn't have said the things he'd said to her tonight if he didn't mean them.

So if she was having difficulty believing him, she realized, it had more to do with her and what had been ingrained in her by her sister and her stepmother and by Dean.

Realizing that, she still found it difficult to grasp that this man—this amazingly handsome, sexy man— could be in love with her.

"Say it again," she whispered.

"I'm in love with you," he repeated, once more speaking slowly and clearly, as if they had a bad phone connection.

And for no reason she understood, at that moment Terese remembered what he'd said to her sister about her earlier—things he hadn't had to say—and it struck her that in Hunter she'd found someone who saw her as a whole person, inside and out, and that he liked what he saw. She realized that was what she'd always yearned for—not to be desired because she had some kind of super-model beauty, not to be sought after because of her trust fund, but to be wanted for all she was.

"You're sure?" she said.

Hunter laughed. "I've never been more sure of anything. Not finding you there waiting for me with everyone, knowing that you were gone, put a hole in me. That only happened for one reason, Terese, because I love you."

"I love you, too," she said, for the first time allowing herself to admit it. Allowing herself to feel it completely.

Hunter closed the small distance that separated them then and pulled her away from the desk into his arms.

He looked into her eyes and grinned even as his brows arched in what appeared to be amazement. "A baby?" he said with laughter in his voice.

"A baby," Terese confirmed, also allowing herself to feel the full joy in that for the first time.

"I knew we made magic that night, I just didn't know how much," Hunter said.

He kissed her then, sparking magic again as that initial kiss went quickly from chaste to heated.

Passion erupted without regard to the turmoil that had brought them here, or to where they were or to whether it was wise.

Passion brought Hunter's fingers to the buttons of her sweater to make quick work of unfastening them.

Passion urged her to slide his jean jacket off his broad shoulders and toss it aside.

Passion put her hands on the hem of his sweater and caused her to interrupt the hungry play of mouths and tongues to pull it off over his head.

Passion took them to the rug in front of the hearth,

shedding the rest of their clothes along the way before Hunter lowered her to the floor and let his hands relearn every inch of her body while she let hers roam every inch of his.

They made love right there in the library, aware of nothing but each other, needing nothing but each other, coming together with abandon. And if Terese had any lingering doubts that she was what Hunter wanted, that she was all he wanted, they didn't survive the hot, steamy explosion that rocked them both when their bodies joined as if one had been carved from the other. The passion that had started the kiss sent them both soaring higher and higher and higher…

And when it was over and they lay with arms and legs entwined, their naked bodies gilded in fireglow, Terese knew one thing for certain—Hunter's arms were where she really belonged, where she really wanted to be.

"I love you," she said, kissing his bare chest before resting her cheek on that same spot.

"I love you," he said. "And I want you to come home with me tonight. I can't wait until after our wedding to have you there."

Terese tipped her chin upward to look at him. "Are we getting married?"

"Yes, ma'am. What'd you think I was askin' you?"

"I don't recall you *askin'* me anything," she said, teasingly mimicking him.

"Want me on one knee?" he offered.

"That would require me moving and I don't know that I have the energy for that."

"Okay, pretend I'm on one knee, then." He cleared his throat. "Terese Warwick, will you take my hand in marriage?"

What flashed through her mind was that she'd take his hands anywhere she could get them. But what she said was, "Yes, I will take your hand in marriage."

"And will you come away with me to my not-quite-a-mansion and be okay living a simple ranch life?"

"Please," she said as if requesting just that.

"And will you help me raise your nephew and our new baby and maybe a couple after it?"

"Only if I can wear the tiara every other Sunday," she joked.

"With the Pretty Princess as his mother, Johnny is liable to make you wear it every day."

Terese smiled as it occurred to her that this man and his son made her feel as pretty as the Pretty Princess.

"But for now," Hunter said then in a deep, drowsy voice, "how about if we steal just a little catnap before we pack you up and take you home?"

"Maybe just a little one," she conceded.

But as Hunter's eyes drifted closed, Terese didn't feel a strong tug toward sleep. Instead she just wanted to lie there beside him and bask in her good fortune.

Bask in the knowledge that she loved this man and that she knew he loved her.

In the knowledge that she loved Johnny and that now she would never be without him in her life.

In the knowledge that she was going to have a baby.

In the knowledge that although it was still a little hard to fathom, she'd somehow found what she'd always wanted and never thought to have—a wonderful man and a family all her own.

* * * * *

Turn the page for a sneak preview
of the next
emotional LOGAN'S LEGACY *title,*
THE BACHELOR
by award-winning author Marie Ferrarella
on sale in October 2004...

For a second after she exited the cab, Jenny stood on the curb, looking up at the tall edifice before her. The building that was owned by and housed the Logan Corporation. With effort, she gathered together the last drops of her courage. She needed all the help she could get.

Despite her last appointment running over, she'd made it to the Logan Corporation building with a few minutes to spare.

All the way over to the shining thirty-story edifice she had practiced what she was going to say to Eric once she was alone with him. But, unlike when she was preparing to deliver summations in court, no amount of rehearsal seemed to improve her performance. The moment she went through her arguments, they melted from her brain like lone snowflakes lying out on a June sidewalk.

He was just a man, she told herself as she rode up the elevator to his floor. Two legs, two arms, one body in between to hold the limbs together. Beneath his tanned skin he had the same skeletal structure as millions of other men.

But oh, that skin, Jenny caught herself thinking. And grew warmer.

This thinking was going to get her nowhere. Worse, if she wasn't careful, it would lose the auction a potential and incredibly desirable bachelor. The fewer bachelors, the less money would be raised. Any fool could see that having Eric Logan on the block would raise the organization a very pretty penny.

There were no two ways about it. She had to think of him as just another body.

Focus, focus, she ordered herself as she stepped off the elevator and walked down the hallway to the inner sanctum that was the gateway to his office.

His office lay just behind the massive double doors. As the VP of Marketing and Sales for the Logan Corporation, Eric occupied an impressive suite.

She presented herself to the keeper of the gate. "I'm Jennifer Hall. Mr. Logan is expecting me."

The woman smiled distantly but politely, then checked a list before her.

"Yes, he is," she replied coolly. "If you'll come this way." Rising to her feet, the secretary led the way back. She knocked on the door, then turned the knob, opening the door just wide enough to allow Jenny to slip through. "Ms. Hall to see you, sir."

Nodding her thanks to the woman, Jenny crossed the threshold. When the door closed again behind her, Jenny concentrated on not sinking to the floor in a heap.

She looked like the personification of efficiency, Eric thought as he rose to his feet to greet Jenny. Every strand of light brown hair was pulled back and in place, except for one wayward wisp at her right temple that had seemed to have rebelliously disengaged itself from the rest.

It made her look more human, he thought, his eyes sweeping over the rest of her. Jordan's sister was wearing a pale gray suit that appeared to be just large enough to hide her figure.

Was there a figure beneath all that, or was she shapeless?

Didn't matter one way or another. He reminded himself that this was his best friend's sister and not another conquest to be won over. This was strictly business, not pleasure. If anything, he was doing a favor for a friend.

"Sit down." He gestured toward the comfortable chair before his desk.

"Thank you for seeing me."

The words were uttered slowly, distinctly. She wasn't enunciating so much as trying to work around a tongue that felt as if it had swollen to three times its normal size. Sitting, she leaned her briefcase against the back of the desk and placed her hands on either armrest, praying she wouldn't leave damp streaks on them. Her palms felt as if they were more than one half water.

Taking a deep breath, she launched into her campaign, fervently hoping she wouldn't sound like a blithering idiot to him.

"I realize that your time is precious, Eric—" She could call him Eric, couldn't she? After all, they did go way back, technically. "But this is a very worthy cause." Her palms grew damper, her speech rate increased. "Since 1989, PAN—that's the Parent Adoption Agency—has been able to help—"

Was she trying to convince him? he wondered. He was under the impression, after talking to Jordan, that this was a done deal. "Yes."

The single word pulled her up short. She felt like someone slamming on the brakes and skidding back and forth along the road, trying not to hit something. "Yes?"

Was there something he wasn't getting? Or had Jordan failed to tell her that he had agreed to this? "Yes, I'll be part of the bachelor auction."

Maybe this time they'll make it down the aisle

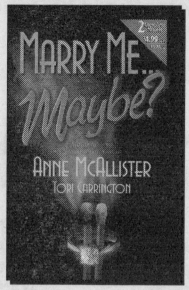

USA TODAY bestselling author

ANNE MCALLISTER

AND

TORI CARRINGTON

The attraction continues to spark in these two full-length novels in which two couples are reunited after several years. The feelings haven't changed…but they have! Is a future possible?

Coming in September 2004.

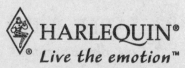

HARLEQUIN®

Live the emotion™

www.eHarlequin.com

BR2MMM

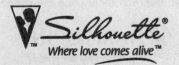